*To: Mauri[ce]
Enjoy!*

## JORDAN MURRAY

# I DID IT FOR YOU

A NOVEL

I DID IT FOR YOU

I DID IT FOR YOU. Copyright © 2022 by Jordan Murray.

This is a work of fiction. Names, places, and events are either the product of the author's imagination or are used fictitiously. Any resemblance to actual persons, places, companies, or events is purely coincidental.

All rights reserved, including the right to reproduce this book in any form whatsoever. Without written permission from the author, this publication and its parts may not be reproduced, scanned, or transmitted in any form, digitally or printed, except in the case of brief quotations embodied in reviews.

ISBN-13: 978-1-7771060-3-4

Published by JM Books

Cover design by Jordan Murray via Book Cover Zone

Interior graphics by Jordan Murray

First printed: July 2022

10 9 8 7 6 5 4 3 2 1

For Ethan.

# THE MAN

*The man sits alone, in the dark. He wonders, over and over again.*

What have I done?

What have I done?

What have I done?

What have I done?

What have I done?

*He did not mean for things to go so far. He should have stopped at one, he knows that. But he could not. The urge was insatiable, it still is. However, it is the lesser of two evils. He must do these bad things to keep him from doing another bad thing, an even worse thing. And he cannot let that happen. Especially not now that she knows. She saw him kill one of the girls.*

*Bess, was her name?*

*Yes, she was pretty, that Bess. Her eyelashes were long, and her lips were full. The man was interrupted, though, because he was caught in the act. Caught by the person who started this all.*

Can I erase what was seen? *the man thinks.*

Can I erase what has been done?

*The answer to the man's questions, or at least to the latter question, is yes.*

*He knows that it can be erased because he has erased it six times so far.*

# THEN

June 9th, 1963
9:30 pm.

It's like the first time all over again, but better.

Tonight, it's Sylvia, another girl from out of town. Brown hair and blue eyes, an unexpectedly beautiful combination. We had dinner together at the diner around the block, and now I'm taking her home with me. I tell her jokes, and the sound of her laugh echoes through the neighbourhood. Sylvia's laugh is infectious and almost makes me want to laugh along. Almost.

## I DID IT FOR YOU

Once we're home, we watch television for a bit, snacking on popcorn and occasionally sipping on Coca Colas. We're having a blast, but then I see the time and suggest that we go to sleep. "I'm tired," I tell her.

I know Sylvia doesn't want to hit the hay at 9:30 pm., but she's the type of person who's selfless, even for someone she just met. I love that about her.

I lead her upstairs into my bedroom, and she falls asleep quickly. I don't, though. Truth is, I'm not tired at all, but I know I need to rest. So does she. We have a big day ahead of us tomorrow.

Sylvia snores lightly and I smile because she looks so innocent when she sleeps. I stare at her in the dark, admiring the way her bottom lip pouts like a fish while she dreams. Is she dreaming of me? I don't dream because I don't go to sleep.

Sometime after midnight, I creep out of bed and open the door, maneuvering myself swiftly around Sylvia; not that I really need to be careful, anyways. Sylvia is still fast asleep, thanks to the sedative I slipped into her Coke downstairs.

\*\*\*

I'm alone in my bedroom now, waiting for Sylvia to wake up.

I'll know she's up because I'll hear her. The whole house will hear her, which is why it's a good thing I'm alone.

When Sylvia awakes this morning, she'll be in the basement. Scared, bound by chains, enveloped in the darkness. Skin flushed with fear. Blue eyes open wide, waiting in anticipation for what comes next.

# NOW

March 22nd, 1970
6:28 am.

I don't need an alarm to wake me up because today is important.

Today is the day that I make my pitch. I don't bother eating any breakfast. Instead, I opt for my default morning nourishment – a cup of coffee. I sip my drink periodically at the kitchen table and read over the wad of papers in front of me, stealing glances at the sunrise out of my rickety window. I rehearse what I'm going to say for what's probably the tenth time this morning. Maybe more. Every time that I stumble on a word or stutter, I force myself to begin again, from the top. I finally finish an adequate run-through of my pitch and take a moment to breathe. It's quiet.

I don't have a boyfriend or husband, someone that I can fall asleep with and wake up next to in the mornings. I'm alright with that. I also don't have a roommate to help pay the rent, and I'm fine with that, too. I do have a cat, though. His name is Candy, and he's a tuxedo cat; he always looks like he's wearing little white boots. I found him near the dumpster behind my building after walking home from work last year. He was only a kitten then, five or six months old at the most.

When I came across him, he was a walking skeleton. A bundle of skin and bones gnawing on a candy wrapper, of all things. He wasn't scared of me when I kneeled at his level and tried to pet him. The kitten pranced over and nuzzled my hand, meowing. I'm not a nurturer, I never have been. I don't have a maternal bone in my body or a desire to protect people, but despite this, I decided to take Candy home with me. We have a mutual agreement of cohabitation. I feed him and clean his shit, and he occasionally lays on my lap, providing me with conditional company. It's a win-win for both of us. And I usually appreciate the quiet. But this morning, I could do with some noise from him. From anything or anyone, really. The silence amplifies the million thoughts dancing about in my mind and I want it to stop.

So, I run through the pitch again and again and again.

# NOW

March 22nd, 1970
9:04 am.

I know something is wrong before I even set foot in my office.

My supervisor, Jane, is waiting outside the door to my office, filing her nails. Somewhere on our level, a printer jams as I'm on my way over, and a few of my coworkers rush to fix it. It's producing some God-awful sound that makes me wince with every step I take. I make my way across the floor, the churning of the machine intensifying, and watch as more employees flock to the perishing printer.

"My article!" a man shouts.

"Someone stop this thing, it's ruining our projects," screams another.

Serves them right. They're both misogynist pigs who've made a move on just about every woman in the company, except me. I think my intensity threatens them. I hide my smirk by turning my face away from the scene as I pass it by.

I arrive in front of Jane, and like any good boss, she doesn't look up from her obnoxiously perfect fingernails and cuticles. I didn't see her look up when the machine started malfunctioning, and she's not looking now, even when I'm standing in front of her. Bitch.

It takes Jane a few seconds to finally acknowledge me. "Sylvia, how are you doing?"

There's something off about Jane's voice, the smoothness in which she speaks. Jane's baseline way of talking is barking orders, and I've never heard her speak this way. My mind starts racing laps.

"I'm doing great!" An exaggeration, but I have to at least appear as if I have it together. "And how are you this morning? I'm really excited to share this pitch with you today. I think I'm really onto something here."

A pause ensues. A pause that's so awkward, my stomach churns like that broken printer, which, from the sound of it, they still haven't come close to repairing.

"You're a good writer and a hard worker, so I won't degrade you with small talk. It hasn't been a good year for the paper. Not just for us, but for newspapers in general. The higher-ups determined that they don't have enough to fund this many employees anymore. They're going to be letting some people go, mostly those with the lowest seniority. Sorry, Sylvia, but since you've only been working with us a year, you're one of them." Jane sighs and steals a glance at the fingernails she so desperately wants to file again. Then she adds, "It's nothing personal."

I've been working for the paper since I moved to Toronto when I was eighteen, so I know she's bullshitting me.

"When do I have until?"

I curse my blunt desperation the moment the question leaves my mouth, but it's the only thing I manage to verbalize.

"You can collect your personal belongings from your office, and after that, you'll have to go. As of right now, you're no longer an employee of our publication."

Jane yawns obnoxiously and resumes her fingernail maintenance, signalling the end of the conversation, if you can even call it that. God, I want to jab that nail file into her eyeballs. But I can't let things end this way.

"Jane, please," I beg, more desperation manifesting in my voice. "I need this job. More importantly, I need to pitch this idea to you. Please," I try again.

"No, Sylvia. It's been decided, the damage is done. The changes have been made. Get your things and go home."

"*Please*." I hate this word. "Let me present the pitch. It won't take more than five minutes, and if you don't like it, then I'll leave and won't ask again. Just give me this chance, I've worked so hard on it."

Jane looks around the floor once or twice before grunting and gesturing towards her office, opposite mine. She takes off quickly across the floor and I follow close behind. Once we're inside, Jane plops down behind her desk, reclining her feet, while I find my place standing in front of her.

"Okay, I originally had diagrams and samples of my questions, but we'll skip all of that for now," I begin, hurriedly. "What's the first thing you think of when I say the word 'murderer'?"

The question is rhetorical but Jane answers anyway with a shrug. "Evil."

"Right. Evil, monster, death. The words aren't pleasant because the people behind the actions aren't pleasant, either. But I want to challenge that narrative with this piece. I want to travel to prisons and penitentiaries across Canada and interview criminals; the worst of the worst. I want to look them in the eye and ask them questions that no one else has the guts to. I don't want to know how they killed their victims, and I don't even care why they did it. I want to understand them, as people, on a deeper level, so that I can understand their crimes. As I mentioned previously, I have sheets of sample questions for a variety of convicted felons in Ontario, Quebec, and British Columbia, along with the logistics of the prisons they're doing time in and the duration of their sentencing." Taking a massive breath to calm myself, I lean my palms onto Jane's desk and look at her. "With this piece, I want to change the way people look at murderers. Or, at least, make them reconsider their position on the matter."

I can tell instantly that Jane isn't having it. Her face is overly expressive with disgust or outrage. Maybe a bit of both.

"Sylvia," she starts, "these people are monsters. They're behind bars for a reason. They're caged like animals, *for a reason*."

"No, you're wrong." I cut her off without meaning to.

Jane subsequently cuts me off, too.

"I allowed you to present this dog-shit idea to me and you wasted five minutes of my very, very valuable time. And now, you're going to listen to my feedback, whether you like it, or not. Whether you agree with me, or not."

I say nothing and allow her to continue. Then, Jane softens her voice slightly, as if she regrets being so stern.

"As I said, these people are monsters. They're sick in the head, and I don't want anything to do with them. The paper certainly wouldn't, either. And if you do, Sylvia – if you're looking to garner sympathy for these people, then I don't know what to say. What exactly are you trying to prove, here?"

"I'm not trying to prove anything."

"Why else would you choose such a twisted topic? Seriously, what's your angle? Couldn't you have written about the upcoming election or the city's pothole project? There has to be more to this than wanting the public to 'reconsider'. Because if you're serious about this project, if you really think these monsters deserve another fraction of a second in the spotlight, then maybe you need to be in one of those cages, too."

"Fuck. You."

I haven't been this pissed in years. I feel like peeling off each one of her fake nails with pliers and forcing her to swallow them. Jane just smiles and nods her head towards the office door. She was never going to consider my pitch in the first place, I know that now.

I leave, making a point to stomp my feet and slam the door on the way out. Jane opens the door and follows behind me, watching as I enter my office across the hall. I don't dare turn around to look at her, nor do I look at anyone else who might have witnessed that scene. I just want to go home. Entering my own office, I turn the lights on and sit down at my desk for the last time. It's starting to register now, my being unemployed. My being a failure at the only thing I'm good at. I don't know what to do next, so I weigh my options.

What would Mom do? She'd probably tell me to cry

and beg for my job back, which is way too degrading for me to even consider. I'm already embarrassed enough by my reaction to Jane's comments. Warranted, in my opinion, but only in my head. I shouldn't have said any of that out loud. I don't know why I did.

What would Dad do? In his fatherly way, he'd tell me that everything will be alright. That's what he always used to say. It was his answer to everything, his catchphrase. When I was seven years old and split my knee open, he crouched down next to me and said it. Every time I came home crying because I got a bad mark on a test, he would say it again. And when our dog, Noodle, died, guess what he said? He told me that it'd be alright. But he's not here to tell me that anymore.

I glare at the stack of untouched papers in my satchel, and they glare back. That's what it feels like, at least. I could have made it big with this piece, finally climbing the ranks of the publication. I've been here for years, writing the same mundane shit over and over again. I want more. This piece is dark, but it's so unprecedented that I thought they'd have to accept it. I feel that I've grown enough as a writer to take on a project like this one, too.

My eyes begin to water at the thought, so I blink vigorously and start throwing things in my bag. Eventually, the papers are covered, shielding me from their accusing stare.

A soft knock at the door quickly erases my almost

tears. My office door opens, and I know it's him. Damian, my other boss. Who I sometimes sleep with. I don't know what we are. I also don't know what will become of us now that I'm fired, if there even is an us. Maybe he's coming here to end it.

"I'm so sorry." The apology comes out of his same gravelly voice, but there's another layer to it. Sincerity. He lowers his voice and steps toward me. "I didn't know until this morning. Who they were laying off, I mean. But even if I did, I wouldn't have been able to stop it."

"It would be too risky," I reply.

"It would be too risky," he agrees.

I look him in the eyes for the first time since I'd last seen him, and a bad idea pops into my head.

No.

I will not ask Damian to get me my job back. He just said it himself. He can't, and even if he could, he wouldn't want to risk it. I shouldn't even want the damned job back. Jane made me look like a fool, and the paper obviously wouldn't have wanted to publish my piece. They don't deserve a writer like me.

I stand up from my desk and continue packing. Damian gently closes the door behind him but leaves it open a crack. He walks over to my desk and picks up a glass paperweight, examining it in his hands. It's shaped like a dog, and my father gave it to me years ago. When Damian gives it to me, his hand lingers a second longer than it should, sending a spark through my body.

"Can I come over tonight?"

The question catches me by surprise, but I promptly recompose myself.

"That depends on the reason for your visit, *Mr. Ward*."

"I want to talk, and we can't do that here." I nod curtly and throw some pencils in my bag. Then he lowers his voice to a rasp and whispers, "We can talk. Perhaps among other things."

When I look at him, we're both wearing the same smirk. He nods in my direction, and we leave it at that. Damian exits, closing the door behind him.

I pack up the rest of my things in a hurry and leave, too. I maze my way through the floor, avoiding eye contact with my coworkers, and, more specifically, any sympathetic stares they might give me. I reach the entrance to the main stairwell and look around, one final time. They still haven't gotten that printer to stop malfunctioning, and no one has thought to unplug it from the outlet in the wall. I hope it sets the whole building on fire.

Before I begin heading down the stairs, I slow and take a look at my watch.

9:25 am. It's been one hell of a day.

# THEN

June 10th, 1963
*8:30 am.*

I smile when I hear Sylvia's first scream.

I'm not happy because she's afraid, but rather, because she's awake. I just can't wait to speak with her again.

Opening the basement door, I walk softly down the steps, hearing her chains clink and clank violently on the cement floor below. Trying to break out, no doubt. But when Sylvia sees me coming toward her, she stops struggling. Instead, she scrambles forward and begs me to let her go.

"Please, please!" she shouts.

I wish she would stop yelling and just smile. She has no reason to, but I still wish that she would. She's just so pretty when she smiles.

Her pleas are met with my blank face and silence. I assess the sight in front of me, keeping a mental log. Sylvia's brown hair is slightly tangled now. She's sitting with her knees pulled up to her chest, trying to hide. From what I can see, she is also quite dirty from sleeping on the cement floor. And – are those scrapes I see? Yes, on her feet and up her legs. She's been trying to get out, clawing at the chains that decorate her ankles. Sylvia sees me looking at her wounds and shimmies away, into a corner.

"You know I can't let you go, Sylvia."

She starts to cry, and that crying quickly evolves into sobs. She screams "Why?" and "Please!" another ten or so times before finally quieting down.

I pull out a chair from the boiler room and drag it towards Sylvia so that I can sit down with her. Try to cheer her up, maybe. I settle the chair just far enough from Sylvia so that she can't reach me through the length of the chains, but still close enough for us to bond. A face-to-face connection.

Sylvia is beautiful. I didn't look at her too closely last night since it was dim in the diner and dark at home, but I'm looking now. She has this little leaf-shaped mark on her upper left arm. Fitting since we're in Canada. She's also got a beauty mark on her face, like Marilyn Monroe.

I'm focusing too much on the wrong things, so I reset my mind.

"I'd like to get to know you more, if that's alright with you."

I ask this with a kind look in my eyes, hoping to gain her trust. In return, she scoffs at me and turns away, but I continue my efforts anyway.

"Not even your favourite colour? Come on, now. What's your favourite colour? I bet I can guess it," I begin. "I'm saying it's…pink. Am I right?"

Sylvia stares past me, focusing on the wall and not saying a peep. I wait five or so minutes before I decide to give her some space. Feeling a tad defeated, I get up and start dragging the chair to the storage underneath the stairs. It'll be easier to access here than having to go to the boiler room every time I come down. I'm about to toss the chair when I hear a noise. Was that Sylvia mumbling something? I think that's a mumble. She said something. I turn around to face her, and to my delight, she's finally facing me, too.

"What was that?" I inquire.

"Blue," she mumbles again, slightly more discernibly this time. "It's blue."

"That's great. Blue's a good colour. Now, don't you want to know what my favourite colour is?"

"Not really."

"It's black."

"Black isn't a colour."

I get quite a laugh out of this. Of course, black is a colour. It's just as much a colour as the blue she so favours.

"How about food. What's your favourite food?"

She pauses before answering, and this time when she speaks, she speaks clearly. Quietly, but clearly. "Vegetables," Sylvia states. "Corn, lettuce, brussel sprouts. That sort of stuff."

"I have to say, Sylvia, that's a little weird. Who in the heck likes brussel sprouts?" I joke. "Anyway, I'll make sure to bring you some vegetables tonight for dinner, then. Aren't you going to ask me what my favourite food is?"

"What's your favourite food?" she asks, sarcastically. I like her attitude. Sylvia can be feisty when she wants to be. A little firecracker.

"Meat." I turn around and begin walking up the stairs before she can answer. I'm halfway up the steps when I shout down, "I'll be having you later for dinner."

I don't mean it literally. But maybe she'll think that I do mean it like that. Or maybe she won't.

Either way, it's some food for thought.

# NOW

March 22nd, 1970
6:20 pm.

It's just starting to get dark outside when I hear a knock at my door.

"Why, hello, there," Damian says, as I let him in.

"Hello, there." I guide him through the doorway and see that he's brought food. "Really? Pizza?" I ask, eying down the box.

"What's wrong with pizza? It's cheese, your favourite."

"Nothing's wrong with it. It's just funny seeing a well-dressed man in my dingy apartment eating a slice of only-cheese pizza." Damian looks down at his slate gray suit and his cheeks redden.

I sit down on the couch, and he does the same, placing the pizza box on my coffee table. He flips the box open and pulls a slice out.

"I wanted to look my absolute best for you," he emphasizes, gobbling down a slice.

"What do you mean?"

"My suit. You said I was well-dressed, and I just wanted to look sharp for you, that's all."

I give him a stare that says, *I call bullshit*.

"Alright, I came straight from the office," Damian admits. "I had to stay late to reprint half the floor's work this week since it got eaten in the Great Printer Jam of 1970. I guess work isn't really the best thing to talk about, though."

"It's fine." And it is fine.

In the hours after getting fired, I started reading a new book (Nabokov's *Lolita*; I'm enjoying it so far), ate an entire pack of cookies (chocolate chip), and took a four-hour nap (on my uncomfortable, creaky couch). Pathetic? Maybe. The only thing missing is a stream of tears flowing down my sunken face, but I refuse to cry. Before Damian came over, I put on a touch of makeup to brighten the bags under my eyes, but it did little to hide the exhaustion. I may look like hell, but I'm feeling much, much better.

My phone rings, perking both mine and Damian's ears. I don't need to answer to know that it's Mom. Probably calling to tell me about her neighbour's sister's friend's divorce, or something of the likes. Damian quizzically darts his eyes from my disinterested expression to the phone and back to me again, but I let it ring.

"So," I begin.

"So," he retorts, staring at the phone while it rings a final time.

We're quiet for a moment before I lean in and kiss him. Damian kisses me back and my body implodes with desire. I lean into him, an invitation for more, but he pulls back.

"Not now… I'm not in the mood."

My face is blank, and Damian looks down in what I can only assume is guilt. Embarrassment forces my legs to stand up and walk to the bathroom without saying a word. I get inside and lock the door, and then I flip the toilet lid down so that I can sit.

Shit.

Once again, my eyes are watering, but I don't let myself cry. I squeeze my eyelids shut and ball my fists, gripping the air in anger. Deep breathing has never done much for me, but I try it again anyway. Surprise, it doesn't work. I continue balling my fists in anger until I feel drops of blood in my right hand. My nails have somehow dug into the palm of my hand, and specks of blood stain my skin. I'm interrupted when I hear a thud from the living room, followed by what sounds like papers being shoved together.

Ignoring my embarrassment, I rush out the door and see Damian on the floor, scrambling to pick up dozens of sheets of paper. A purse is tipped over beside him. It's my purse. My papers.

"What are you doing?"

"I-I'm sorry, I was just going to read a page to see what it was," he stammers.

I cross my arms. "Well, what did you think?"

"I don't know what I thought I was doing. I'm really sorry. I'll put it all back in order, I promise. And then I'll get out of your hair."

"No, I mean, what did you think of my idea?"

He finishes gathering the papers and sets them on the table, and asks, "Can I be blunt?"

"Always," I respond.

"I think it's brilliant. It's unique, and I've never seen anything else like it in the media. Not as in-depth as you want to go, at least. I think you've got to go after this, you've just gotta. But I have one question, and I'm serious. Who the hell hurt you so badly that you came up with this?"

I smile.

# NOW

March 22nd, 1970
6:55 pm.

The food Damian brought over has now gone cold. Too much talking, not enough eating.

"You thought that the paper would green-light this piece? Sylvia, it's good, but it's too jagged."

"Well, it doesn't matter anymore." I turn away from him. I don't like the look Damian is giving me, and I'm still mad at him for rejecting me. I don't even know why he did it, either, since he gave me such a pathetic excuse.

"No, it does matter. I think that it has potential, but not for a newspaper. It's too big an idea. I think you should do it on your own. You could write something, publish it yourself."

"On my own? But what would I even do with it all when I'm done?"

"A book." Damian's face lights up. "You write a book about it. Do your interviews, write your thoughts, and use the excerpts and research to write something that will shock the world."

Tempting. "No, I can't. I couldn't. I don't even have an outlet to do the interviews anymore. The paper fired me, I'm not a member of the press. How would I get into the prisons?"

"I'll take care of that."

"What do you mean, 'I'll take care of that'?"

"You still have your press badge, don't you? When you go in and they take the employer info from you, just put down my name and telephone extension instead of Jane's. The press pass will probably be good enough but put me down as your employer. Just in case."

"You're sure about this?"

"Yeah, but you're the one who needs to be sure about it."

I'm not sure, but I've already dedicated so much time and effort into creating the foundation of this piece. I owe it to myself to see it through, so I nod my head, causing Damian to smile

"Okay," he says. "I want you on a plane first thing tomorrow, though. I'll take you to the airport and buy you a ticket if you don't have the cash right now. This could be big for you, Sylvia."

"No. It *will* be big for me."

"Confidence. Zest. That's the Sylvia that I know and love."

Damian winks at me but then gets up to leave.

Why the hell would he stand me up like that and then joke about loving me? Why show me so much support for my writing when he rejected me five minutes earlier?

"Well, I should get going now. But I was serious about driving you to the airport tomorrow. If you want me to, that is."

"Thanks. I think I'd like that." We smile at each other and leave it at that. Damian goes home and leaves me alone with my thoughts.

Love.

This isn't the first time that he's said it, but it's the first time that I've really listened. I've always been hesitant to have a relationship with Damian. He's asked me before, and I've said no. I blamed it on our work and said it wasn't appropriate to have a full-fledged romantic partnership with my boss. He countered my point by asking how it's appropriate to have casual sex with him.

I've always known that he's into me, but I didn't think he was serious. I like Damian, sure. But I'm not interested in a real relationship, and he knows that. Yet, for some reason, he sticks around. Maybe he thinks he can change my mind. I don't love Damian and I probably never will, especially not after he embarrassed me like that. I don't love or trust anyone, and that's just the way it is.

Damian's only been gone half an hour when my phone rings again, and this time I answer. Mistake number one.

"Like hell you are."

My mother's frustration is almost tangible through the telephone when I vaguely tell her about my plans. Mistake number two.

"They'll be short trips, and I don't really have a choice. My boss is making me go. Everyone else has a family or husband or wife, and they can't go out of the province. That only leaves me." Lies, they come too easily to me. When she doesn't respond, I tack on, "And I'll come home in between trips to visit you. At home."

"I'd prefer it if you weren't jetting off across the country."

"And I'd prefer it if I kept my job." Another lie, but she doesn't need to know that I got laid off yet.

"When do you leave?"

"Sometime tomorrow. I'm not sure when I'll be coming back, but it won't be too long."

"I need you close to me. I don't have anyone."

She's trying to guilt me, but it won't work. Not this time. Silence hangs between us, and I've had enough of her shit for today.

"Alright, Mom, I have to get going now."

I put the telephone back on its base, ending the call before she has a chance to respond.

My stomach gurgles and I realize that I haven't eaten anything for hours. I didn't have any of the pizza Damian brought, and he took the leftovers with him when he went home. I settle on making breakfast for dinner, a fine-dining experience of stale pancakes and orange juice.

After the food's ready, I sit down and eat, my face contorting at the first dry bite. The pancakes are chewy and bland, so I look in the refrigerator for maple syrup. There isn't any syrup in there, nor is there much of anything else. I really need to get some groceries.

Straightening my posture in the stiff kitchen chair, I finish the pancakes and swallow my last gulp of orange juice. I'm tired, but I can't go to sleep yet – it's only 7:00 pm., so I decide that it's time to work. The chair creaks as I stand up. So does the floor. Everything in this damn apartment creaks, I swear.

I walk into the living room and sit down at my desk, choosing to prep for the first interview. I feel almost giddy bringing out my notes and paperwork, laying them out on the surface for me to admire. My desk looks like a mess with all the papers and scraps, but it's organized. It's all there. Candy is lounging around on the desk, too, getting fur all over the place. I swat him away so that I can get to work.

When I first got the idea for this project, I decided on three people. Three is a respectable number, I think. It's enough to be a challenge, but not too much of a workload. Three people; three individuals imprisoned across the country for the most unpleasant of crimes. Those who make the front page of the papers for the dirty details of their crimes, but not for who they are as people. Because contrary to what we might like to believe, they are people.

No other major newspaper has done anything so risqué, let alone any reporter or writer on their own. The thought of doing this by myself scares me, but the excitement I feel at the prospect of writing my very own book trumps that fear, tenfold.

Staring at my papers, I re-read the list of names I've already memorized. At the top of the list is Walter Gordon, a man in his forties convicted for the first-degree murder of his wife in 1963. I don't have to travel far for this first interview since I'm barely leaving Ontario. The prison that holds him is only an hour-long drive from Montreal, so I hope to be there and back in two or three days.

Walter Gordon currently resides in the Special Handling Unit of a federal penitentiary, and once I make the appointment, I'll have only 15 minutes to interview him. Family and conjugal visits are granted more time, but people in the media aren't given that privilege. We're vultures, and even the prison officials know it.

I pull out a newspaper clipping from my Walter Gordon case file and examine it for any details I might have missed reading it through the first dozen times. The picture accompanying almost every story covering Gordon's crime shows him being escorted up the steps of a police station in cuffs, a cold expression on his face. He is surprisingly handsome, or at least he was when this photograph was taken. Walter Gordon is in his early forties now, a self-made widower rotting away in prison. There's nothing in the newspapers that detail his motive for murder – just that he was the one behind it. I scrawl some more questions in my interviewing notebook and slump back in my chair.

Exhilaration and exhaustion course through my body at the thought of being face-to-face with a killer again.

# THE MAN

*When the man was just a boy, he wanted to be a policeman. He wanted to help make the world a better place, to lock away the bad people.*

*He never imagined that he would become one of those bad people.*

*He never imagined that this is why he would become one of those bad people.*

\*\*\*

*When she was just a girl, she did not know what she wanted to be. Like the tide, her aspirations changed often, along with her mood swings. On Monday, she would want to be an artist, only to decide on Tuesday that she wants to be a veterinarian. By Sunday, she would have gone through at least a dozen careers.*

*Mood swings still plague her now that she has grown.*

*The man hates the mood swings.*

*The man hates her.*

*The man loves her.*

# THEN

June 10th, 1963
*12:07 pm.*

"Are you going to kill me?"

I pay Sylvia no attention to this comment about murder. She hasn't the slightest idea of what's going on here. I find her assumption insulting.

It's lunchtime now, so I continue setting up our food and cutlery in the basement. I make sure to give Sylvia a plastic fork with blunted edges. As promised, I made her the brussel sprouts she's so fond of, but I had to go all the way to the market to get them for her. She better eat them. I also made peanut butter sandwiches and brought down some milk. I also hope she's gathered that I won't, in fact, be eating her for lunch or dinner.

After I finish setting the table, I sit down to face Sylvia.

"So," I say, "what else do you like to eat? I need to know these things so I can make you happy during your stay here."

"You can make me happy by *letting me go*," Sylvia shouts, enunciating the last three words with conviction and tenacity. It's a breath of fresh air from her predecessors, who typically gave up in a fit of tears the moment they awoke in the basement.

I shake my head with a chuckle.

"Sylvia," I say, "you know I won't do that."

The plate of food I had so generously made goes flying from our makeshift table and I discover that Sylvia has made a mess. I bend over and begin tidying the food on the floor when I feel something wet on the side of my face. Touching my cheek, I feel drops of saliva.

She spat on me, that ungrateful wench.

I stand up and flip the table with a force I hadn't yet shown to Sylvia, until now. I didn't want her to see this side of me, not yet, but the circumstances demanded it. She must know that this behaviour is not acceptable.

I take two steps forward, and Sylvia scoots off her chair and onto the floor, scurrying back into the corner. I continue my advance towards her, squatting down to her level once I arrive. She must see something in me, an anger that she didn't know was there, because she's scared. Petrified, is more like it. Sylvia is more fearful now than ever before.

Sylvia refuses to make eye contact with me. I remedy that by pinching her chin between my fingers and forcing her head upwards to face me.

"Listen here, you little shit. I went to the trouble of making you a lunch, and a lunch with one of your favourite foods, at that. And how do you thank me? With a level of disrespect that will *not* be tolerated. Are you listening to me?" I let go of her face and she nods her head. "Good. You know, I don't have to feed you. I don't have to be this kind to you, so don't do anything like that again. Don't even *think* about it."

I get up to leave and see Sylvia's body slouch back in relief from the tension she was holding in. I swiftly spin around and slap her hard across the cheek, the sound echoing off the concrete.

"*Screw you!*" she screams, in my face.

I turn around to face her a final time before retreating upstairs.

"I liked you, Sylvia. I thought you were different from the others, I really did. But now, not so much. You'll regret the day you were born when I'm through with you."

# NOW

March 23rd, 1970
9:23 am.

It's my birthday today, the anniversary of the day I was born, and I'm celebrating by hopping on a plane to Montreal.

Damian drove me to the airport at 6:00 am., an hour and a half before my flight time, and dropped me off with an awkward hug. Neither one of us bothered to exit the car. I didn't tell him it was my birthday because I don't tell anyone about it. Besides, today isn't about me.

It's about Walter fucking Gordon.

It was surprisingly easy to be granted an interview with a murderer under the guise of my old job. As Damian said, I still have my press identification from when I would go on site for stories, instances which were far and few between. That badge is getting some use now. Answering some questions over a telephone call and faxing over a copy of my badge was all that was required of me to gain access to Walter Gordon. I gave the officials the number of my *supervisor*, as well. I have Damian to thank for the idea, and for covering my ass in case anyone gets curious.

This is the first step toward the next chapter in my career. I'm going to be the author of an unprecedented, all-access dive into the psyches of some of the most notorious criminals in the country. Maybe my old newspaper will review it in their What To Read This Week column, which, funny enough, I helped to write.

I grab my luggage from baggage claims and make my way to the exit, maneuvering through a sea of people. There are signs in French everywhere I turn, and only some of them have English translations. I don't speak a lick of French aside from your average *bonjour* and *au revoir;* a consideration I probably should have made before visiting a bilingual province for the first time.

As I step out of the airport and breathe in the frigid air, I also realize that I didn't dress warmly enough. The snow has already melted back home, but the Winter season is still very much alive in Quebec.

I hail a taxi and have him drive me to the nearest hotel, where hopefully I can change into something a tad warmer. I won't be outside for long on this trip, anyways. My interview visit with Walter Gordon isn't until tomorrow at noon, and I'll probably stay in my hotel room until then.

"Have you been here before, miss?"

The cab driver has a thick French-Canadian accent, and I'm silently grateful for the fact that he speaks English. He also looks a bit like Santa Claus.

I smile politely, buckling my seatbelt.

"No, it's my first time."

He mumbles in agreement, scratches his white beard, and begins driving, returning his focus to the road. Just moments later, we arrive at a small motel. It looks shabby, but it'll do.

Before exiting the car, I pay the driver and give him a handsome tip because I'm feeling particularly kind today. Then, I grab my luggage from the trunk and wave him goodbye.

"*Au revoir! Bon voyage, mademoiselle*!" he calls out.

I wave again, not sure what to say in return.

\*\*\*

The mattress is as stiff as a board when I sit down — there may unironically be a wooden plank under here.

I check my watch and see that it's only 11:00 am., which is unfortunate. I have a lot of free time and nothing to do with it. So, I sit up and dial my mother's number into the telephone on the nightstand. She picks up on the first ring.

"Hello?"

"Hi, Mom, it's me."

"Oh! Sweetie, happy birthday! I phoned you earlier today but there was no answer. Were you at work?"

"Yes, I was at the office for a few hours, but they let me go home early, being that it's my birthday and all."

The lie leaves my mouth so smoothly that I believe it. I'm impressed, but not surprised.

"Why, isn't that kind of them. You better thank your boss tomorrow. What are you doing to celebrate? Would you like me to treat you to a nice dinner?" Her enthusiasm wears on my conscience a bit. "Or you could come home, and I could make you some lasagna and a cake, maybe. Chocolate or vanilla, whichever you'd like. How does that sound?"

"That sounds nice, Mom, but I can't."

"Oh, that's alright then."

To my surprise, she doesn't pry more than that.

My mother and I haven't ever had that bond everyone is always talking about. When I was younger, we didn't go shopping together. I didn't help her with sewing or cooking or housework, and although she'd tried to teach me everything she knew, I never quite took to the domesticity. I much preferred doing things with my father that most little girls didn't do, like hunting and hiking. We had a special bond that I think my mother always envied a little. It wasn't quite jealousy, but I think she wanted a relationship with me like what my father had. As her only child, I can understand why my aversion would have been a slap in the face, both when I was younger, and now. The fact is, Dad's gone now, and I'm still keeping a distance from my mother.

"Well, I'll let you go enjoy your special day, then," she says to me.

"Mhm, I have some things I need to do."

"But before you go, I did have a question." I remain silent, beckoning her to continue. "I'm thinking of selling the house. There are too many memories, and there's no need for a house so large when I'm here all by my lonesome most of the time. It's just too much upkeep, and I think it would be for the best. I don't know where I'll go just yet, but maybe somewhere right in the city. But I wanted to ask if you would come over and help pack some of my things with me, or at least, go through your old bedroom and see if there's anything you want to take with you. In the guest room, there are some things that belonged to your dad, too. I don't know why I still have them after all these years. I suppose in some ways, I miss him."

I pause, processing the information she's just shared. Selling the house is one thing, but this is the first time my mother's expressed that she still has feelings for my father. If she still has a room for his stuff, she must have always felt this way.

"I wish he didn't have to get sick," Mom continues.

"It's not like he chose to be sick," I counter, a bit too defensively.

"I know." She sighs. "Anyways, I'd appreciate it if you'd come over and help sometime soon. Whenever is convenient for you. Alrighty, well, happy birthday again, dear. Talk soon. Love you."

I hang up the phone.

# **THEN**

June 10th, 1963
*12:21 pm.*

I'm not alone.

There's a knock at the door, and for a moment, I fear that Sylvia will hear it and scream for help. But the knocking ceases, and so I tiptoe to the window, peeking through the blinds to see who was there.

A little boy skips down the disheveled

walkway, pulling a red wagon full of newspapers behind him. When he reaches the main road, he turns left and continues on to the next house, which is a long, long walk away. I'm filled with relief, but also, fear.

What if it had been someone else, like a neighbour or Sylvia's family? No, I'm being ridiculous. There aren't any neighbours for at least a mile, and Sylvia's family doesn't know where she is.

Nobody does.

# THEN

June 10th, 1963
3:15 pm.

I'm lounging on the sofa when the telephone's shrill ringing pierces my ears. I don't want to answer it, but I should. And I do.

"Yeah, I'm doing good. No, I haven't been out much. Yes, I've been making sure to eat. No, I haven't tidied the main floor yet." I try to answer as quickly, and calmly, as possible. I twirl the telephone cord between my fingers, willing the conversation to end. I still can't believe there was a telephone booth all the way out there for him to use.

To bookend the call, I ask when he'll be coming back, to which the reply is, "The day after tomorrow."

We hang up, and I spend the rest of the afternoon watching television. I try reading a book but can't focus well enough on the words, and I don't know why. I'm all alone in the house, there's no one here to infringe upon me and my guest. The main floor and upstairs are quiet, with not a single noise anywhere. This is what I want, but it's almost lonely.

My ears perk at the sound of Sylvia from below and excitement rushes through me. I go over to the basement door, which is closed, and, of course, locked. I hear muffled noises from Sylvia. I hear her screams, cries, and the sound of chains smacking against the concrete, reminding me of a comforting fact: I'm not alone.

# NOW

March 24th, 1970
11:59 am.

Nobody cares that criminals are people, too.

The reality of our world is that it's easier to dehumanize murderers as monsters because the alternative is too difficult to comprehend. Not many people can wrap their heads around why a man would just up and kill his wife, so they don't bother trying. Maybe they don't want to understand – or maybe they *do* understand and don't want to face themselves.

Perhaps they, too, have had fleeting thoughts about slipping a sedative in their boss's morning coffee or bludgeoning their husband's trashy mistress. But they don't want to acknowledge their capacity to act on primal rage. They don't want to relate to murderers, robbers, or bombers; the worst the world has to offer, even though those *monsters* are just like them. Human. The realization that criminals have feelings, lives, and people that love them would contradict the portrait society has painted. Despite having family and friends and feelings, most cannot sympathize with them because their actions outweigh their humanity. The media assures that the stories of their crimes are heralded to the world, and in the process, strips them of their identity in place of a simple label: a monster. This is what happened to Walter Gordon.

It's been difficult to obtain information on Gordon's motive for his crime, as he's never gone on the record to explicitly confess. At his trial, about half a decade ago, Gordon pleaded not guilty to the murder of his wife, Christine Sheffield, in the first degree. Everyone knew that he murdered his wife, though.

The evidence presented in court was indisputable and the case was a cakewalk for the prosecution. A clerk at a local hardware store witnessed Gordon purchase two containers of Arsenic and testified as much in front of the judge. Those containers were later found, empty, in the Gordon kitchen garbage, shabbily covered up with a banana peel and a few packages of cigarettes. In using the revolutionary forensic toxicology Marsh Test, Christine Sheffield's cause of death was determined to be fatal ingestion of Arsenic Trioxide. Rat poison.

Locals rejoiced when Walter Gordon was found guilty and convicted of murder in the first degree.

Other than some basic information on Walter Gordon, this is the extent of his public presence. My file lacks any specific details on Gordon himself as it relates to the case. I don't even know what he did for a career before murdering his wife. I know his actions but not his reasoning, and I'm hoping to change that today.

I step out of the taxi and begin walking up the winding path that leads to the front prison gates. At the outer security checkpoint, I show them my ID and press badge and allow them to pat me down. After the guards clear me, I'm ushered inside the building, and I repeat the demonstration of my credentials and subject myself to a pat-down once more. I pass, again, and begin my journey through the penitentiary.

The guard looks weary as he brings me through a series of secure corridors, but he doesn't say a word. We soon arrive at the visiting center, and I take my seat.

"He'll be out in just a few minutes, Miss," says the guard.

I smile politely and nod my head in thanks. I then turn my attention to the divider in front of me. It's not quite glass, but not quite plastic, either. There's a chip at the end of this divide, and I lean closer to examine it. If this was someone's attempt at breaking themselves out of the slammer, then it was certainly a pathetic effort.

Then I see him.

Turning the corner, two prison guards appear, escorting a handcuffed Walter Gordon to the visiting station. The moment he sees me, we lock eyes. His brown eyes are warm and inviting, while mine are cold and gray.

"Hello," he says to me, taking his seat. I don't bother returning the greeting and instead cut to the chase.

"Let's get started, shall we?"

## THE MONTREAL EXAMINER

September 5th, 1963

# MAN OR MONSTER? WALTER GORDON ARRESTED IN GRUESOME MURDER

On September 1st, 1963, Christine Anne Sheffield was found deceased in her Montreal home by a neighbor. The police were called and an investigation was launched. Sources say that multiple bottles of rat poison were discovered at the residence.

Sheffield's husband, Walter Gordon, was nowhere to be found. When he returned home later that evening, Gordon was arrested for the murder of his wife. He is now in police custody.

The investigation is ongoing.

# NOW

March 24th, 1970
12:18 pm.

The interview begins.

He doesn't look like he did in that picture, and not just because he's older. Gordon's face is jaded and miserable, while his body is slouched like a sack of potatoes.

"Mr. Gordon," I continue, "my name is Sylvia St. James. I'm going to be the one interviewing you today. Is that alright?"

It doesn't matter if it's alright or not, but it doesn't hurt to start building rapport.

Gordon smirks. "I didn't know they were sending a woman over."

"Does it matter that I'm not a man?" I inquire.

"No, no. I'd prefer you to be a woman. We don't see many of those around here." He howls with laughter, looks around the room, and then stops. "And what a pretty little thing you are. You remind me of my wife, got those same grayish eyes."

I begin writing my observations, starting with the unsettling, but not completely false, comparison of his deceased wife and me.

After a moment to consider, I decide to use it as a launching point.

"Speaking of your wife," I say, "do you think she was a good-looking woman?

"Well, you could say she was easy on the eyes, I suppose. Nothing too special, but she wasn't ugly. Now, let me guess. You're going to ask why I did it."

"Actually, that's not why I'm here today." Gordon doesn't respond, so I go on. "Your case headlined local newspapers for most of 1963. Any average Joe who bothers to do a bit of research can find out how you murdered her and what evidence was used to convict you. I know all that already, but I want to know more about you. I want to know about your childhood, your personality, what you like and what you don't. What makes you tick."

"In other words, you're interested in me and not my crime."

"I'm interested in how you got to that point, the point of killing your wife. I'm also interested in how you perceive the world and those in it. We'll begin by poking and prodding into your childhood. What was your life at home like?"

I prepare my pencil and paper.

Gordon sighs and then begins. "Guess we'll start with childhood, then. That's what you want, right?"

"Yes, that's what I just said."

"Well, alright then. No need to get snippy. My mother was home with me and my brothers, and Pops was an automobile salesman. Things were alright, I guess. Never got beat or anything like that, if that's what you're asking."

"You said your 'Pops' was a salesman and your 'mother' stayed at home," I interject. "Your wording leads me to think that things weren't always the best between you and your mother. Would you say that's accurate?"

"Well, now, aren't you a smart cookie. She stayed home and cared for us kids while Pops went out to provide for the family. And what does she do when my older brothers head off to college? She invites our next-door neighbour, Bobby Fitz, over for a good time while Pops is at work and I'm at school. I saw them through the window one day coming home from class. She's a God-damned whore, and Pops deserved better."

I might be onto something here. "That must have been tough for you. How old were you when this started happening?"

"Must've been about thirteen or fourteen when I found out about them, but it could have been going on for longer."

I ask if his dad ever found out the truth, to which Gordon responds, "I didn't have the heart to tell him. I wanted my mother to fess up and tell him herself, but she never had to. Got hit by a drunk driver when I was sixteen."

"I'm sorry to hear that."

"I'm not."

Gordon turns his head and pretends to be occupied with looking at the cement wall. I clear my throat and catch his attention once more.

"Tell me," he begins, "what's a pretty lady like you doing interviewing someone like me, huh?"

In my most professional voice, I say, "I've already told you about the purpose for this meeting, and-"

"Yeah, yeah. You want to take a peek inside my brain or some shit like that. But isn't this strange for someone like you? Shouldn't you be off cooking for your husband or shopping for some lipsticks at the department store?"

"Listen, we aren't here to talk about me. End of story. Now, what was your career before being incarcerated?"

"I was an automobile salesman, just like Pops. Same place and everything."

"And how many serious relationships had you been in before your marriage with Christine?"

"Just one. Her name was Linda. I called her Lindy."

I scribble the name down.

"How long were you romantically involved with Lindy? What was she like?"

"I figured you'd want to hear about Christine, not some old flame. We were in the same homeroom class in the eleventh grade, that's how we met. Dated for seven months and two and a half weeks."

"That's quite specific," I note, writing the numbers down and underlining them several times.

"She was the first girl to go steady with me. Lindy had hair so blonde that it was almost as white as snow, and she was always kind."

"And what happened to the relationship, Walter?" I question, intentionally switching to using his first name.

"She died."

"How did she die?"

"Poisoning, they say."

Gordon does something unexpected. He looks into my eyes and his mouth twitches into a smile, as if he didn't just say his first girlfriend died in the same way he was convicted for killing his wife.

He starts humming some disturbing tune while I take a dry gulp of air. One of the guards on the inmate's side peeks around the corner to tell us we only have one minute left, and I nod.

"So, Walter, is it fair to say that you're a pretty reserved guy? From what you've told me, it appears as if you don't like conflict. Not only do you dislike it, but you actively avoid it. You followed in your father's footsteps not because you wanted to, but because he likely pressured you into it and you caved, not wanting to disappoint him. Being that poison was your modus operandi, I think that you never had the guts to face your conflicts head-on. You took the coward's way out, with both your relationships, it seems. Too bad you're only in here for the one."

Gordon is scowling at me now, and I take a mental note of everything that he does. The guard approaches and begins to stand Gordon up while I say one last thing.

"You couldn't even expose your whore of a mother for fucking the neighbour."

I stand up and head towards the exit.

# THE MAN

*"Are you coming in, hun?" the man's wife asks.*

*"In a second," he replies.*

*The man is sitting outside of the tent. He sits on the grass, staring out at the sun as it retreats below the horizon. Just a few feet away, the man's wife prepares to go to sleep within four angled walls of polyester and nylon.*

*This was a great idea. This trip, this visit. He wishes things could always be like this. Happy, peaceful. The way things were before* she *came. The man knows that he should not blame her, but he does.*

*Why does he blame her?*

*How can he* not *blame her?*

*"Hunny?" the man's wife calls again.*

*She peeks her head outside of the entrance to the tent, a flimsy flap of fabric.*

*The man looks at his wife. He thinks that she is beautiful, there is no doubt about that.*

*The man does not do this because he finds the girls attractive. He is certain of that fact, at least. Though, if he is not attracted to them, then why does he do it? The man does not know. He suspects it is because of her. Somehow, it always comes back to her.*

*The man stands up from the grass and begins to walk towards the tent. His wife smiles at him, her head still poked out of the flap. The man loves the way his wife is smiling at him right now. She has not smiled like this in a long, long time. It makes the man happy. The sound of chains clanking also makes the man happy. And muffled screams. And the feeling of holding a life in his hands.*

*And the feeling of taking that life.*

*"Coming, sweetie."*

*Happiness is such a fickle thing to understand.*

\*\*\*

*The man and his wife are in the tent.*

*They are supposed to be on a romantic vacation – if you can call camping a vacation, that is. The man does not have many means to live by. His wife stays at home, and he works a regular 9-to-5 office job. This is the best he could do for their wedding anniversary. He remembers the date but not how many years they've been married. The man has had other things on his mind lately. For quite some time, actually.*

*This anniversary trip is not for them. It is selfish. The man needs this weekend away, just the two of them, to get out of his head and to get out of that house.*

*Away from her, and away from the temptation to act again. To kill again.*

*The man and his wife are kissing, but there is no*

*passion between them. At least, not from him. The man cannot stop thinking about how she is doing. He would like to hurt her because she hurts him in existing, in simply breathing. He still cannot articulate why that is.*

*The man's wife stops kissing him.*

*"Is something wrong?" she asks.*

*"Just thinking," he responds.*

*"Am I thinking what you're thinking?" asks the man's wife, with a flirtatious giggle. They begin kissing again, the woman intent on taking things to the next level.*

No, *the man thinks,* you are not thinking what I am thinking.

*For the first time ever, the man is thinking about killing his wife, too.*

\*\*\*

*The man and his wife sleep together.*

*They had not had sex in years, another consequence of having* her *in his life. The man did not particularly enjoy it because he was thinking bad thoughts the whole time.*

*Afterward, they get into their sleeping bags and prepare for bed.*

Something feels off, *the man thinks.*

*The man is uneasy but cannot quite place what the source of his worry is.*

*He thinks that maybe, the thoughts about his wife are a byproduct of this mysterious stress he is feeling. The man had never thought about murdering his wife until tonight. She had always been excluded from his compulsions.*

*Why now?*

*Why start tonight?*

*The man tosses and turns in his makeshift bed, his wife already sleeping soundly beside him.*

*He thinks and thinks until his brain cannot think anymore.*

*Then, a revelation comes over him.*

It must be her; *the man thinks.* She must be doing something; I can feel it in my bones.

*The man does not sleep that night, but rather, he*

*prepares for the great possibility that he will finally kill her and end things, once and for all.*

# THEN

June 10th, 1963
*Afternoon*

Before Sylvia, there was Rita.

Rita had golden-brown skin and the darkest eyes I'd ever seen. Her hair was equally as dark, and it was in an intricate braid when I first saw her. She was sitting on the park bench, gazing at the sky and playing with a loose curl that managed to escape the binding of her hair tie. She looked positively radiant.

I made sure to survey her for a bit, verifying

that she was alone, before approaching.

I knew that she was from out of town and that she was only in the area to visit an old friend, who ended up flaking on her. After realizing her friend wasn't coming, Rita wandered over to the park. Together, these things made Rita the perfect subject.

I'd done this maneuver a few times by then, and there was no shred of worry in me as I sat down beside her.

"Hi," I said to her, smiling.

She looked away from the sky and greeted me, albeit with hesitation.

"Oh, hi."

There was a pause, and I almost feared that the awkwardness would ruin my opportunity. *No*, I thought, *I'm unsuspecting. I've done this many times before and will do it many times after. Go for it.*

"What's your name?" I asked.

"R-Rita, what's yours?"

Luck was on my side because at that moment, it began to pour rain. The clouds in the sky had become black, the sun retreating behind them.

"I live just around the block; we can go

inside for a bit. Just to get out of the rain."

It wasn't a question, but a command under the guise of hospitality. Rita nodded her head, and then I nodded my head.

We both sprang from the bench and started to run, Rita following my lead. Our feet were soaked before we'd even left the proximity of the park, but we didn't care. Rita was running towards somewhere dry with a new friend, and I was doing my job. There was a smile on each of our faces as we ran and laughed, but for many different reasons.

"It's just around the corner, up here," I shouted over the rain, pointing in the direction of the house. In reality, our house was still a way off.

It's not really our house. We own it, but we don't live there full-time. "Don't mix business with pleasure," he always says. It's too late for that.

We moved away from the subdivision surrounding the park and turned onto a rural strip of road. After a few minutes, the pavement withered away to rocks and dirt. After another few minutes, the houses that surrounded us on our way over were replaced with fields and a vast landscape of grass.

I slowed down as we neared the road to the house and turned around to see Rita. She'd also stopped running, and I gestured for her to follow me up the path. She didn't speak another word as I unlocked the front door and held it open for my guest.

Rita stepped inside and didn't even have a chance to scream before a pair of hands reached out from behind the door, smothering her face with a cloth infused with chloroform. Rita collapsed to the ground.

I picked up Rita's feet and helped drag her to the basement.

\*\*\*

Before Rita, there was Laurel.

From what I had observed during my reconnaissance, Laurel was not a very nice girl.

She'd spat on another girl's shoes when they bumped into each other at a mini-mart, and there was a permanent scowl on her face. Laurel was unpleasant to spy on and even more unpleasant to be around. She was tricky, at first.

## I DID IT FOR YOU

When I met her outside that mini-mart in the next town over and asked her to come home with me, she initially declined. Her decline was in the form of an obnoxious laugh. She'd expected me to go away after being denied, but I stayed. I'm persistent like that, I have to be.

Standing there, watching her, I noticed how restless she was, always bouncing her legs and fiddling with her hands. Pairing these actions with what I'd seen of her behaviour, I made an informed guess.

"I have some smokes back at my place if you want some."

Laurel's eyes, thick with black liner, were immediately filled with excitement. It was the most animated I'd ever seen her throughout the four days I'd been watching her.

"Hell, yes, I want a smoke," she'd exclaimed. "Let's go."

Laurel began marching ahead of me, not even knowing where *my house* was. She was such a know-it-all. A brat. Later that day, I was especially eager to contribute to her death and dismemberment.

In the end, Laurel never got her cigarettes.

The truth is that we don't even have smokes at the farmhouse. I don't condone it.

Smoking can cause death, after all.

\*\*\*

Before Laurel, there was Bess.

Bess was my first. Not his first, but mine. Ours, together. I didn't scout her out like Sylvia or Rita or Laurel, and I didn't kill her, but I did assist in dismembering her body.

He wasn't supposed to be at the farmhouse that afternoon. I went there thinking that I would be alone. It was a hot day, and I wanted to take a dip in the pond on its property. I'd unlocked the front door and entered, beginning to undress, intent on heading straight to the water. Noises stopped me, though.

I felt the muted bumps and bangs through the walls and floorboards just as much as I heard them. The house is old and so is everything in it; the walls and floors are paper-thin.

At first, I couldn't make out what those sounds were but eventually determined that they sounded like struggling.

Following the noises, I'd crept across the floor and opened the door to the basement, ever so slightly. When I took the first step onto the wooden stairs, there was a creak. Not loud but audible enough that the sounds of struggling below stopped abruptly. My feet were glued to the stairs, unable to move.

Then he came into view.

"What are you doing here?" he said to me, with a nervous smile. He oozed artificiality.

I didn't respond, and instead, made my way down the remaining steps and turned the corner once I had fully descended.

There was a girl tied to a chair, duct tape on her mouth. Her head was slumped over to the side in an unnatural position, and there was blood pooling out of a slice in her neck. It was as if someone had drawn a smile with the blade of a knife as their pencil, the incision going ear to ear.

I turned around to see him sneaking up on me. He was probably going to kill me because I'd discovered his secret hobby. But before he had the chance, I made a proposition.

"I can help you; you know. If this is something

you do often, and, from the looks of it, you probably do, I can help you find them. Girls. Talk them up, bring them home. And you can do the rest. I promise I won't tell."

# THEN

June 10th, 1963
*Afternoon*

Before Rita and before Laurel and before Bess and before all the girls before them, there was me.

There was supposed to have been me.

# NOW

March 24th, 1970
12:37 pm.

I drag myself out of the prison with my notepad in my purse and ideas swirling around in my mind. I wish I didn't have to leave so soon.

I catch a cab and request to be taken to the motel. After retrieving my things and checking out with the front desk, I catch another taxi and head towards the airport. This driver isn't as kind as the one I had previously, and not as personable as the Santa Claus driver that picked me up at the airport yesterday. He's cranky and doesn't say a word to me the whole time.

We drive in silence, and when we arrive at the airport, he simply turns with a huff, gesturing for his payment. I'm barely out of the taxi cab before he's speeding away. Asshole.

I head inside and purchase a one-way ticket from Montreal to Toronto at Pearson International Airport. After crossing security and checking my bag, I start towards Gate 2. While waiting in the lounge for my flight, I seek out a payphone and decide to call Damian. I'm eager to tell him about the Walter Gordon interview, and I make a conscious decision to ignore what he did the other night. He's my business partner now, not my romantic partner.

I insert my coins into the dirty slot and pick up the receiver. Damian answers on the second ring.

"Hey, it's me," I say.

"Sylvia, hi. How's everything been going out there?"

"Good. Great, actually. I finished up with the interview earlier today and I'll be on a plane home tonight. Listen, I'd like to run what I have so far by you and get your opinion on it all. Damian?"

"Sorry, I'm at work right now." He's distant, off somewhere far away in office-land. "That sounds great though, yeah."

"Alright, well-"

"We could meet for dinner tonight if you'd like. You

can tell me all about the interview, and your plans."

His voice is sincere, like he truly does feel bad about being distracted just now. Good, he better feel guilty.

"I'd like that." I check my watch and see that it's almost time to board. "I gotta catch my flight now, but I'll be ready for dinner. Pick me up at 7:00 pm.," I instruct, hanging up the phone.

I grab my purse and get in line to board the plane

\*\*\*

All I can think about the whole trip home is Walter Gordon.

I didn't mean what I said at the end to Gordon, but I said it anyways because I needed to see how he'd respond. My experiment worked, and I don't feel guilty about having hurt his feelings. If anything, it only proves that he *does* have feelings.

Gordon was just a teenager, a child, when he was exposed to his mother's infidelity. Only a few years later, his mother died suddenly and tragically, which must have left him confused. Was he supposed to feel sadness? Anger? Happiness? Maybe he felt them all, or maybe he didn't feel anything at the time.

As I look out the cubical window of the plane and stare at the clouds, I hypothesize that maybe his mother's death was the advent of the Walter Gordon we know today. Or, rather, the societal perception of Walter Gordon as a criminal, a monster. While he may be a murderer now, he was also once a child. A child who was mistreated and betrayed by his mother; a mother that he later lost in a car accident.

I'm not making excuses for him, but these are the simple facts.

Walter Gordon is not a monster – he is human.

# THE MAN

*This trip is supposed to last three days and two nights.*

*It has been just over one day and one sleepless night, and the man is ready to go home. He cannot bring his wife with him when he goes. And the man's wife will not let him go without her. He will have to be sneaky, get away from his wife and take the truck before she notices he is gone.*

*Could he go in the middle of the night, the dark sky as his cover? No, the man is big, and she would hear him get out of the tent.*

*Could he send her off somewhere on a meaningless task, and then leave once she is out of the vicinity? That could work, but where would the man send his wife? They are in the middle of the woods. The nearest town is miles away, in which case, she would have to take the vehicle. But the man needs the vehicle, so this option is out of the question.*

What else, what else? *the man thinks.*

*The man's wife beckons him over for an early lunch. She has set up some snacks on an old picnic table that was already at the camping grounds when they arrived.*

*The man is hungry and decides to come back to his conundrum later, with a full stomach.*

# THE MAN

*Later that afternoon, the man decides to incapacitate his wife to escape the campsite.*

*The man does not wait for his wife to go to sleep. Instead, he strikes her from behind while she is tending to her broken sandal strap. The man drops the rock almost in unison with his wife's body dropping to the ground.*

*The man wastes no time in retrieving the car keys from the tent and hopping into the truck. He knows exactly where he is going.*

# **THEN**

June 10th, 1963
*5:50 pm.*

Sometimes I don't feel human.

The first time that we did this, it didn't feel wrong. It was new and exciting, a secret we could bond over. Being his assistant was something I took pride in, something I could do for him; but now, I've taken things into my own hands. I, the protege, had assumed a role of dominance, and I'd done so without the knowledge or approval of my teacher. He's not my teacher, though. I like to think of myself as self-taught.

Upstairs, I finish making dinner for Sylvia and me. She doesn't deserve it, not after what she pulled earlier, but I figure I should feed her anyways. It's what he always does.

I transport our meal in a picnic basket this time because there are more components to it than there were at lunchtime. There's bread and butter, corn, some beef, and two pieces of apple pie for dessert. If she doesn't piss me off, that is.

When I open the door to the basement and make my way down the stairs, I hear chains clinking together.

"Hi," I say, taking the final step into the basement. "It's dinner time. Are you hungry? You barely ate your lunch, so I can imagine that you're quite hungry."

Sylvia simply nods her head in response.

"Great. I'll start setting the table, then."

I admittedly don't put as much effort into the spread as I did at lunch; not if there's a chance she'll ruin it, again. After everything is in order, I sit. I don't give Sylvia a chair because she deserves to sit on the ground after all the disrespect she's shown me.

"Let's dig in."

I give Sylvia her food but don't give her utensils this time. She begins to pick away at it with her dirty hands but does so slowly. She has to be starving by now, so I don't know what her issue is with me. I eat my food right away and savour every bite. Doing all this is quite laborious, and I'm hungry.

The ground beef reminds me a bit of ground flesh. I only tried it once, the last time we did this, but I've wanted to try it again, ever since. He doesn't know that I ate a piece of the last girl, and he won't ever find out.

Besides, Sylvia is too thin for that, and she hasn't been eating, either. I don't know how I would go about doing it. I don't even know where to go from here, but I'm running out of time to decide. I won't be alone here much longer before he's back. He always comes back.

As if reading my mind, Sylvia asks me what my plans are.

"If you're going to kill me, why don't you just

do it already? Just get it over with."

She spits the words at me like venom. I can't really blame her.

"I don't know yet." I pause. "Eat your food."

We continue in silence, the only sound being the scraping of my plastic fork as I play with the scraps on my plate. I've finished my dinner but see that Sylvia still hasn't eaten much.

"You know, I was going to give you some dessert if you finished all of your food tonight. You didn't eat much, but maybe I'll give it to you anyways, just so you can eat something. Do you like pie? I have a nice, hot slice of apple pie here, just for you. I can't bake, so I didn't make it, but it's good. I warmed it up and everything."

I reach into the picnic basket to pull out the slices of pie and lay them on the table. Sylvia still doesn't look at me, or the pie, despite me setting it down right in front of her. Instead, her focus is on something else. She faces her head towards the staircase and listens.

I hear the muted sound of a lock being jangled, and then, the sound of a door opening. The front door to the house.

No, I'm supposed to have another day, he

shouldn't be back now. Not yet.

I run as quickly as I can to the other side of the basement to retrieve a roll of duct tape. I need to keep Sylvia quiet. If she hears that someone's home, she might do something stupid and ruin this for me.

"Helloooooo?" I hear from upstairs. "I'm home, where are you at, E?"

I'm not quick enough.

Sylvia looks to the stairs and then to me, staring me dead in the eyes as she screams, and screams, and screams.

# NOW

March 24th, 1970
6:28 pm.

I want to scream when I see my reflection.

After entering my apartment, I head to the washroom and get ready to apply my makeup. But then I look in the mirror and realize that I look like death.

There are deep bags under my eyes that weren't there a few days ago. They likely developed last night; I barely slept at all because I was so excited about the interview. My hair is equally as unappealing. It's wiry and knotted from leaning my head against the side of a plane for two hours. It needs a wash, badly. I sigh loud enough for no one to hear and undress. I'm sore and stiff from the plane ride, and I almost consider taking a bath. I take a cold shower instead.

Afterwards, I dry myself off with a ratty towel and put on the outfit that I chose for tonight. I step into a fitted suede skirt, accented by a black belt with a gold ring, and then pull a brown long-sleeved shirt over my head. All secondhand, of course. I tuck in the shirt and then begin to blow dry my hair, using a brush to flip up the ends as it dries.

My reflection in the mirror is beginning to look more presentable, but I'm not quite there yet. I paint my eyelids with a shimmery champaign shadow and apply a few coats of mascara. There's a knock at the door, signalling the end of my mini makeover.

"Coming!" I yell out, throwing my toiletries and cosmetics into the cupboard below the sink.

I walk quickly out of the washroom, into the hall, and to the front door to see… my mother.

"Oooooo," she gawks, "where are you going tonight, all dolled up?"

"Not now, Mom." I try to peek behind her for any sign of Damian. "I'm about to leave."

"Well, I just wanted to check in and see how you are, since I didn't get to see you on your birthday, and all."

She steps toward me and brings me into her arms for a smothering embrace. I hate every second of it. After about thirty seconds or so, she releases.

"I was also wondering if you could come by tomorrow if you aren't working. To help me pack, maybe go through your old things."

"Yeah, yeah, I can do that." I smile artificially in an attempt to shoo her away. "Listen, Mom, I really have to get going now."

"Hello?"

Damian appears behind my mother, carrying a bouquet of vibrant flowers. I hate flowers, especially as a sign of love or thanks. Flowers always wither away and die, and is that really what you want to symbolize your affection with? No thanks.

Mom whips around in surprise and then turns back to face me.

"Oh, I see," Mom says, with a wink. "I'll leave you be."

"Mrs. St. James, my name is Damian. I'm going to steal your daughter away for dinner tonight if it's alright with you."

"Mrs.-"

"We're running late, Mom. I'll be over tomorrow to help you like you asked."

I slam the door behind me and take Damian by the arm, running him down the stairwell.

"It was nice meeting you!" Damian calls up.

# I DID IT FOR YOU

\*\*\*

The restaurant we're going to is right next to my apartment, so we arrive quickly.

After we've been seated, Damian asks, "What was that all about?"

"I just don't have the best relationship with my mother, that's all. She randomly stopped by while I was on my way out, and I didn't want to keep you waiting." Damian stares at me. "I'm going over tomorrow to help her pack up her house. She's moving."

"Well, that's nice. I think."

The waiter comes by and takes our order; a seafood dish for Damian, and for myself, a medium-rare steak. Since Damian's footing the bill, I'll be indulging myself tonight. When the waiter leaves, we resume our conversation.

"So," Damian begins, "how was it? How was the interview?"

"Thrilling isn't the right word. It was more than that. When I first saw Walter Gordon, it was terrifying and exciting, all at once. Once the interview began, it was even more exciting. I wasn't scared anymore because I was getting an unprecedented insight into his mind. He grew up with his parents and two older brothers, but when his brothers moved away, his mom started an affair with their next-door neighbour. Gordon caught them in the act and resented his mother for it. The father never found out about the infidelity because Mrs. Gordon died in a drunk driving accident before she had the chance to confess. Not that she would have, anyways. After the death, Gordon never had the heart to tell his father about the affair. That secret knowledge has plagued him since childhood. But that's not all."

I pause to take a breath, preparing to share the most shocking information yet.

"I asked about any previous relationships before his wife, Christine. He said that he only had one prior girlfriend, his high school sweetheart, Linda, and he was pretty vague about their relations with one another. He said that Linda was poisoned and died, and he had this smirk on his face while he told me. Then, our time was just about up, so I did something risky. I pissed him off. I said he's a coward who hates confrontation, always taking the easy way out. When things got hard with his partners, he poisoned them; probably one of the most indirect and spineless methods of murder there is. And then, right before I walked out, I told him that he was a coward, that he couldn't even confront his mother about her sleeping with the neighbour. He was fuming. I thought he was going to explode from anger."

With impeccable timing, the waiter comes by to drop off our drink orders. Damian takes a sip of water and then shakes his head with a chuckle.

"After all that I'd read about this guy in the papers, I

didn't know if you'd get anything out of him. But you did, and you did one even better; you might have just connected him to another crime."

"Don't underestimate me, Damian."

The waiter comes by once more to bring us our food and we dig in.

# THEN

*June 10th, 1963*
*6:02 pm.*

I panic and punch Sylvia, burying my knuckles square in her face. She still doesn't stop screaming, even after the impact of my fist.

I rip off a piece of duct tape and she's too busy screaming to wriggle away from me. Her screams are more muted under the extra layer of tape, but I need her to stop entirely.

"What was that? Are you alright?" I hear

from upstairs, over the muffled screams. "Where are you?"

"Coming!"

I turn to Sylvia and stare at her so intensely that she stops screaming.

"I'm going to go upstairs. I swear to God, if you make a sound, any sound at all, I will kill you." She mumbles something. "What?" I ask, before remembering that she has tape over her mouth.

She mumbles whatever it is she's trying to say again, and I decide to tear some of the tape from her face to hear what she has to tell me.

"You're going to kill me, anyways."

Sylvia says this not with sarcasm or spite, but with defeat. I think she's realizing, truly realizing, that she's been abducted and that she's going to die. Without responding, I put the tape back over her mouth and pat it. Entering the fetal position on the floor, Sylvia cries quietly into her knees.

I turn off the light and go upstairs.

# NOW

March 24th, 1970
*9:14 pm.*

After dinner, Damian walks me home.

"Do you know what your next step is?" he asks, as we walk up the stairs in my apartment building.

"I know who's next up on the list, but I don't have any interviews scheduled yet."

"Well, I have one suggestion for you, if you want to hear it, that is. It's not directly related to your book, though."

We stop outside my apartment door, and I fumble in my purse for my keys.

"What is it?"

"I have a cousin. He, uh, killed his parents when he was eleven years old. Our families were never really that close. My dad and his brother were raised in a trailer in Northern Ontario, and my grandparents, from what I've heard, were pretty abusive. Once he turned eighteen, my dad got the hell away from there and never looked back. His brother – my uncle – was just as shitty as his own parents. Basically kept his kid in shackles. He never went to school, never went outside to play. My cousin never knew anything more than pain. I only met him once, when I was in my early twenties and he had just turned eleven. He was so excited for human contact."

Damian looks as if he's going to tear up.

"My uncle probably hit him a dozen times during our visit there. Dad got into an argument with him about it, and in the end, we left. I never saw my cousin again. A few months later, my dad got a call from a police officer telling him that his brother and sister-in-law were killed by his nephew. He was a minor, nothing was publicized, but he's been in a psychiatric hospital for five years now."

"I'm sorry to hear that."

Damian looks up at me and smiles meekly.

"I've been wanting to visit him for a while, now. I don't even know if he'll remember me. But I want you to come with me. Not for an interview, but as my support person. If you're willing, that is. And at the very least, our meeting with Lee might give you some insight into abnormal child psychology and the effects of trauma."

I nod my head, saying, "Of course, I'll come."

He steps towards me and closes the space between us, kissing me deeply. I close my eyes and savour the affection. Finally, our lips break a part, and Damian steps backwards.

"Thank you for being so understanding. I appreciate it. And I'll stop by soon and let you know the time and place once I set it all up."

"Great, I look forward to it." And I really do.

"Well, I'm going to head out then. But I had a great time tonight. Let's do it again soon." I nod my head, once more. "Goodnight, Sylvia."

"Goodnight, Damian."

I step inside my apartment, tossing my purse and the flowers on the floor, my mind already stirring with the interview questions I'm going to ask Damian's cousin for my book.

# NOW

March 25th, 1970
*11:31 am.*

Walking up the driveway to my childhood home isn't as nostalgic as I thought it'd be.

With each step comes a memory, yes, but there aren't feelings that come along with them. Some memories are fleeting, like the vague ones I have of running through the sprinkler on the front lawn. But some of them I can recount in excruciating detail, like the time my father taught me how to ride a bike.

I must have been six or seven years old, and he was helping me learn on our driveway's strip of sloped pavement. My father didn't tell me how to ride the bike; he just sat me on the bicycle seat and watched as I rolled down, down, down the driveway, unable to stop myself. I flipped myself off of the bike when I hit the curb that meets our street, and split one of my knees open in the process. He walked down the driveway and crouched to my level. Though it hurt, I didn't cry, and he didn't say anything to me. He just extended his hand for me to raise myself off the ground, and so I did. After that, I picked up the bicycle and wheeled it back up to the highest point of the driveway. I fell, again and again, five times, maybe more. Then, Dad finally told me the secret to learning how to ride a bike.

"Balance," he had told me. When I asked him what he meant, he'd said, "Only you'll know what balance means to you. It's different for everyone. Your balance will be different from mine or your mother's, as it should be. I can't tell you how to ride a bike. Keep trying, and once you find what works for you, stick with it."

My mother opens the front door to greet me before I even make the first step onto the porch. She pulls me into a warm hug, and I let her do it.

"Well," she says, "are you ready to be put to work?"

I exaggerate a smile, mumbling a polite, "Mhm," and step inside.

## I DID IT FOR YOU

I haven't been home in years, and it seems like Mom found a way to alter every aspect of the house in one way or another.

Different coloured walls; newly stained kitchen cupboards; new decor. In the front hall, where there used to be a large family portrait of myself, my mother, and my father, along with our old dog, there is now an abstract painting hung in its place. The canvas is off-white with varying shades of red shapes and splotches adorning it. This abstract art reminds me of blood spatters patterned sporadically on a surface. My mother sees me looking at it and rambles on about how she won it at an auction in downtown Toronto.

"It's beautiful, isn't it?" she remarks.

I neither agree nor disagree.

"So," I say, looking around some more, "what would you like me to do first?"

"Hm, let's see. I suppose you can go straight into your room if you'd like. I've got almost everything packed except for your bedroom. I didn't want to touch any of your things."

Mom nods in the direction of my bedroom, down the hallway, as if I don't know where it is.

"And here are some bags for anything you want to throw away or take with you." She hands me some plastic garbage bags and I go on my merry way.

My steps creak and moan on the wooden floors from the front hall, all the way to the foot of my bedroom door. I turn the knob slowly, paying attention to the stickers on my door spelling out my name, and it's like I've entered a time capsule. Everything else in the house is so different, but my room is the same, just like she'd said it was.

Baby pink walls and cream-coloured curtains. A twin-sized bed with a canopy, the surface of which is covered entirely in a menagerie of stuffed animals and frilly pillows. Across the room, my matching birch desk and chair are situated against the wall, facing the window, pencils and sheets of leaf paper spread out over the top. There's something eerie about being in here, this bedroom preserving my childhood.

I don't even know where to begin.

I settle on my desk, turning the drawers inside out to see if there's anything important or worth keeping. All I get are old composition books for high school and scrap papers. I find an old science quiz crumpled in the bottom drawer, and when I smooth it out, I see why it was crumpled, to begin with.

My tenth-grade science teacher, Mr. Strank, gave me a C+ on this biology quiz when I evidently deserved a higher grade, so I'd taken out my frustration by sketching Mr. Strank's decomposing corpse. See? I did know my biology.

I move onto my dresser. The dresser drawers are still full of clothes, but nothing that I'd wear now as an adult. I pile the clothes into one of the garbage bags and head to my closet. I forgot that I had kept my bookshelf in my closet, so I'm a bit surprised when I open the door and am greeted with a wall of books.

The shelf takes up almost three-quarters of the closet's already lacking space, and each shelf is packed tightly with books and knick-knacks. I clear the top two shelves and sit on the floor, examining each item and determining its fate. I trash almost all the books that I read for my secondary school courses, which were mostly Shakespeare plays.

Why did I even have three copies of *A Midsummer Night's Dream*? I throw all three of them in the garbage.

That's when I see it, hidden in between a copy of *To Kill a Mockingbird* and *Frankenstein* – the journal.

It's worn and leather-bound with a compass embroidered on the front cover. I don't dare to open it, not now. I'm not even sure that I'll end up reading it, but I throw it in the keep bag, just in case. At the very least, I can make sure that the contents of these pages stay confined to their leather walls. My heart's beating fast at the thought of my mother finding it and flipping through, or anyone else, for that matter. I silently debate my options.

I could burn it, but then I might need it someday for some reason. Probably not, but there's always the chance. I could also keep it hidden away somewhere, underneath a cushion or locked in a box. That way it'd be safe. I decide to go with the second option.

I'd kept a journal throughout my teenage years, but not a typical one. None of that *Dear diary* shit. I didn't write about cute boys or mean girls. I didn't write about my life at all, really. I wrote about what was inside my head, after everything that happened.

I don't want to open the journal and read it, reliving that dark place in history; but I'm also pulled by a desire of ineffable origins to do exactly that.

I quickly pack up the rest of my items and exit the time capsule.

\*\*\*

In my *keep* bag, I have some notebooks with old poems inside, a teddy bear, a bracelet that my father gave me for my fourteenth birthday, and the journal.

I wrap the latter in an old t-shirt, just to be sure that my mother doesn't see it on my way out through the opaque garbage bag, under a bunch of other items. I'm paranoid and protective of the garbage bag I'm taking home with me and feel myself sweating as I struggle to make small talk with my mother before I leave, but she's hesitant to let me go.

"Would you like some coffee, hun? Or a glass of water, maybe?"

"No, I'm fine, thanks."

"I'd really like it if you could stay for a bit longer,"

she says. "It's been so long since we've sat down with each other and talked."

I don't have anything else going on today, so I tell myself that another ten minutes won't matter and that I can make it through if it means maintaining my appearance of normalcy.

"Alright, yeah. I'll have some coffee, then." She looks at me with a motherly scowl until I add, "Please."

Mom smiles and scurries into the kitchen as I lay my garbage bag on the floor and take a seat.

The more I look around, the more I don't recognize this house as the one I grew up in. Everything is so different. I didn't think that I'd care about her selling the house, but I'm starting to feel upset. No, not upset. Am I nostalgic? Sentimental? There's some part of me that longs to be a child living in this house again, with both of my parents, before everything went to shit. I think *that's* what I'm missing.

My mother returns with only one mug in her hand.

"Are you not having one?" I ask, as she sets my coffee down in front of me.

"Me? No, no, no. I barely sleep as it is. I don't need to be up all night. Ha! That's just what I'd need."

She laughs it off, but I know she's not kidding, nor is she exaggerating.

"It's been that way for a while, but you know that already. I'd hoped it would get better over the years, but it hasn't. I've grown lonelier, which has only made things worse. You know, sometimes," she says, then stops mid-sentence.

I look at her expectantly, but she moves her head downwards to face the floor. She speaks the next sentence so softly that the words are barely audible.

"Sometimes, I wish he was still here."

I force myself to sip the coffee, which is still scolding hot, but I need something to fill the moment right now. I don't say anything; I have nothing to say. My mother doesn't speak, either. Then, she mumbles something.

"What was that?" I ask, my tone clipped.

Mom sighs and slowly raises her head to face me.

"I said… I know I shouldn't, but I do."

"You're right, you shouldn't miss him. You shouldn't even think about him. He's gone and we should both be glad. He ruined our lives."

"That's your father, you're talking about, and-"

"I'm aware."

"Do you really blame me? I've been alone in this house for almost a decade. No partner, no child. You treated me terribly when you were young and still living here, and after you moved out, you never came back to visit. You still don't. I call all the time and you hardly answer. When you do, it's like I'm talking to a brick wall. The conversations are one-sided. How is that any way to live, for you, or for me?"

"Maybe that's because I've separated myself from what happened. I've moved on, and you haven't. You're still living in the past, yearning for the same man who hurt us so badly. He got sick and now he's gone. He's not coming back, and you just have to accept that."

"I wonder sometimes if it was my fault, if I could have done more to stop it from happening. How did I get things so wrong?" Mom says, her eyes swelling with tears.

"Do you mean him getting sick? That has nothing to do with you. You didn't cause it, and you sure as hell couldn't have stopped it. Don't flatter yourself by thinking you had that sort of influence."

"I just can't help but think about what life would've been like if all that didn't happen."

"But it did happen, and it happened over half a decade ago. Your home renovation projects, all the redecorating and refurnishing you've done? It's just one big attempt to fake that you've moved on. I'm not here. Dad's not here. No one else comes here. So, who are you trying to convince? Yourself?"

Mom looks up at me now, more anguish on her face than I've ever seen in her before.

"Listen, here," she says, pointing a shaky finger at me. "If you want to talk about faking things, you can't ignore the years you've spent convincing yourself that things are fine. You never spoke to anyone about what happened, not even me. You just moved right along, like you hadn't just had your whole childhood ripped away from you. You lost your innocence that day, and I lost my daughter."

"You know, maybe you're right. Maybe you could've stopped Dad from getting sick, or at least, stop things from progressing as far as they did. I was just a kid. How could I have known the signs to look for? Meanwhile, he did a downward spiral, and it all went under your radar."

I'm pissed beyond words. I know the vile things spewing from my mouth are mostly false, but she doesn't. And right now, this is the best way to hurt her.

I set my coffee mug on the table with a bit too much force, with some drops of liquid splashing onto the table's surface. I stand up and grab my 'keep' garbage bag, ready to leave. We're both silent as I attach the straps on my shoes and start opening the front door.

"I still love you; you know. I'll never stop loving you."

I don't answer; I just slam the door behind me.

# **THEN**

June 10th, 1963
6:10 pm.

I leave a hysterical but duct-taped Sylvia in the dark and go upstairs.

Adrenaline rushing through my veins, I enter the kitchen and close the basement door quietly behind me. I hold my breath the entire time. The kitchen is empty, and for a moment, I think that maybe I imagined it. I haven't gotten much sleep lately, so it's possible. Then I hear his voice and tense with fear, realizing it wasn't my imagination.

He can't find Sylvia, he can't.

I don't know how he'll react to the situation or what he'll do – to Sylvia and to me.

The wooden floors creak under his boots until he is standing in front of me, holding out his arms for a hug.

I step into the smothering warmth of his embrace.

# NOW

March 26th, 1970
*3:02 am.*

I haven't been able to sleep since the confrontation with my mother yesterday.

   I'm laying in bed, staring at the ceiling. I'm hot and kick the covers to the side, but then I'm cold and pull the blanket up to my chin. I do it again and again until I get tired of being restless and sit up. I turn the lights on, walk into the hall, and head towards the kitchen for a glass of water. I'm parched and down three full cups of water while Candy sleeps soundly on the kitchen countertop.

Something about what my mother said yesterday doesn't sit right with me. It's wrong, she got it all wrong. I'm not running away, I'm moving on. Mom thinks that she knows, but she doesn't. She thinks that I'm a traumatized little girl hiding in a grown woman's body. I'm not. She thinks I hate my father for everything that happened. But it's more complicated than that. She thinks that I'm a victim, which is a half-truth.

My mother doesn't know anything.

After I finish my fourth glass of water, I sit down at the kitchen table to do some work because I'm not getting any sleep tonight.

My next interview is tomorrow with a man named Kassem Zhao. He's held at Brockville Jail in – surprise – Brockville, Ontario. He pleaded guilty to one count of first-degree murder and was sentenced to eighty years behind bars. The person he killed is his biological mother, but Zhao was raised by his recently deceased grandmother.

Sitting in prison today, he's even younger than I am. And he would have only been nineteen years old when he committed the murder. Some people have cited in various news articles that Zhao has some sort of deformity or abnormality in his hand or arm, but I haven't been able to pinpoint any information more specific than that. I'll find out soon, though.

That slander from my mother pissed me off, and I'm more driven than ever before to pursue this piece.

AUGUST 1968

# BROCKVILLE
## NEWS

**ISSUE #8**

## SCORNED SON-TURNED-KILLER

Kassem Zhao, an adopted nineteen year-old man from the Brockville area, has been arrested as a suspect in the death of Karen Zhao. Sources say the deceased is the suspect's estranged birth mother.

"I'm appalled at the actions of this young man," says a local resident.

A woman who claims she and Zhao attended the same secondary school calls the latter "a monster" and says, "I hope he rots in that prison cell."

BROCKVILLE NEWS                PAGE 1

# NOW

March 27th, 1970
12:57 pm.

After a three-hour drive to Brockville (and a gruelling security check), I walk into the jail's visiting commons and find my seat across from a young man that, outside of the circumstances, I might have considered handsome.

His posture is impeccable, with his legs politely crossed and his back positioned straight against what looks to be an uncomfortable prison chair. At least the chairs on the visitors' side are padded. Zhao's hands are folded neatly together on his lap, but they're tucked into the long orange sleeves of his prison jumper. Dark hooded eyes meet my gaze the moment I come to face him.

"Good afternoon. I presume you're Miss St. James," he says, matter-of-factly.

His directness is a pleasant surprise. "You presume correctly. And you're Mr. Zhao?"

"The one and only. I wasn't expecting someone like you to be doing such a *twisted* story," he says, making a face.

"What, because I'm a woman?"

"Not quite. Women can be journalists just the same as men. I'm not that archaic," he laughs. "I just think you're too pretty to be dabbling in the minds of criminals."

A smile finds its way across my face, and I catch it too late; he's already smirking in return. I try to hide it behind an artificial scoff, but he sees right through it.

"Alright, Mr. Zhao, shall we begin?" I say, after clearing my throat, in another futile attempt to regain composure.

He leans in ever so slightly and says, "You can call me Kassem, you know. What can I call you, Miss St. James?"

"Nothing, that's fine."

"Okay, Nothing. Hit me with your first question."

Kassem lightly smirks, as if he knows he's being a smart-ass. At least he's self-aware.

"Can you tell me a bit about your childhood? Your family, your friends, any particularly traumatic or joyful experiences that stand out to you."

"Well, my mother was going to give me up after I was born. My grandma took full custody of me so that I wouldn't go into the foster system. My mother dropped me off when I was about a week old, and I never saw her again. Grandma raised me on her own after that." Kassem waits until I finish scribbling in my notebook to continue. "I'm sure you're already aware, but this is why I was cast aside by my mother."

He raises his left arm to me, using his other hand to shove up the sleeve. His left hand is clubbed, the whole of his wrist and hand turned outwards in the direction of his pinkie finger. I try to hide my surprise when I first see his hand but fail miserably. In all the newspaper reports that I've read on his case, there's never once been a photograph of his hand, nor any explicit mention of his condition.

"You don't have to look so shocked, Nothing. You're an intelligent woman, I'm sure you've seen things far worse than a clubbed hand." I nod, beckoning him to continue. "It's called a Radial Club Hand, but most just call it a clubbed hand. I'm missing a bone called the radius. I can't do much of anything with my left hand, which I've eventually come to accept over the years. But it frustrated me a lot as a child."

He takes a breath and continues.

"Grandma always said it made me special and that we shouldn't fix it because of that. In reality, we just didn't have the money to fund such a large procedure, and even if we did, doctors probably couldn't have fixed it entirely. It's not like they can give me a new radius. I appreciate that she tried, though. I guess that's not a single event, but I'd say it's a significant piece of the story. When Grandma passed a few years ago, I had nothing left. I was lost. And now, I feel that way more than ever."

I write some key points in my notebook:

*Speaks fondly of his grandmother but barely mentions his mother; says he's accepted his clubbed hand but initially hid it from me; demeanour is polite and he's well put-together overall – is he making up for something?*

I open my mouth to ask another question, but Kassem speaks first.

"Are you getting some interesting information, Sylvia?" He gives me that boyish smirk again.

I stare at him blankly, wondering how it is that he knows my name.

He leans forward across the table between us and says, "It's on your notebook." I look down at the paper, and so it is.

*Observant: attention to detail*, I write responsively.

"Moving on, then. Did you ever feel like you missed out on not having a mother? Or a father, for that matter?"

"I knew my father died before I was born, but that's all I knew. That's all my grandma knew, too. Neither of us even knew his name. And like you said, I had a mother figure, but I missed out on a real mother. I didn't know anything about my mother. Not her birthday, not her age, nothing. Up until Grandma passed away, I didn't know why I was given up, either. I had always assumed it was because of this," Zhao says, holding up his hand, "but I never had anyone, or anything confirm it."

"So, your grandma never gave you any explanation as to why you were in her custody," I repeat.

He nods.

"Ever since I can remember, she'd told me that my mother wasn't capable of taking care of me. That was the excuse. But I always wondered, 'What if she didn't want me because of my hand?' Or, 'What if she thought I was a disgrace?' Turns out, I was right."

I write his words down, and out of the corner of my eye, I see Zhao tuck his hand farther back into the sleeve of his jumpsuit.

"Alright, I'd like you to walk me through the day of the murder. I don't want to discuss evidence or timelines or anything we already know about. I want to know what was going on in your head, what you were feeling and thinking about when you decided to kill your mother, and then yourself."

I prepare my pencil and paper.

"Grandma had gotten slower, more lethargic. She was nearing ninety years old, and I think she knew her time was running out. The night before she died, she called me into her bedroom, and we had this deep conversation. She finally told me the truth about who my mother is and why she gave me up as a baby. Grandma confirmed that I was given up because of my deformity, only, my mother didn't give me away to Grandma. She was going to just drop me off somewhere. A fire station, someone's house, I don't know. And my mother told Grandma what she was going to do with me when she visited my mother in the hospital after I was born. An argument broke out, and ultimately, I went home with Grandma a week later.

I wasn't too surprised, but I was hurt. And that wasn't the worst of it. That night, Grandma instructed me to retrieve a box hidden in the back of her closet, since she couldn't get out of bed anymore. Inside it were letters, probably a hundred or more, addressed to my mother. Grandma said she'd been writing to my mother for years, sending her drawings I'd made and updates about my schooling, hoping that one of those years, she would want to be involved in my life. All those letters were returned to the sender, and Grandma didn't have the heart to get rid of them. She had me sift through the letters until I found a single letter different from the rest – one from my mother, the only letter she had ever sent in response. 'Ma, I beg you. Please stop with the letters. I don't want them. I don't want him.' Those were her exact words. Grandma stopped sending letters after that. The next day, I found Grandma dead in her bed."

"I'm sorry, that must have been very difficult," I say.

"Yeah, it was. She'd passed in her sleep, and when I found her, it occurred to me that I wanted to die, too. I hadn't quite realized it until that day when Grandma passed away, but I had nothing. I never had any friends, I had never been in an actual relationship, and I didn't have parents. When she died, a part of me did, too. I cried next to her body for an hour before the anger came. It was a rage that was so intense, I'd never felt anything like it before. I went back to the box of letters and dug to the bottom to find the one my mother had written. It had her address on the envelope, and so I went there. I didn't go there to kill her, I only wanted to confront her, but I – it just happened."

A tear rolls down Zhao's cheek and I think it's genuine. I look into his eyes, trying to get a better read on him, just like I did with Walter Gordon. But Kassem Zhao is much different. The eyes that stare back at me are melancholy, and I think that's how they've been this entire time. He uses smirks and one-liners to hide his feelings, but I see him now for who he truly is.

I flip through some court documents and newspaper

clippings that I brought along in my file folder.

"The court believed you had every intention of going there to murder your mother. You were convicted for murder in the first degree."

"That is correct."

"And yet, you pleaded guilty. Did you not assert that it wasn't premeditated?"

"It was just easier to let them have their narrative. I knew I was going to spend the rest of my life behind bars either way, so I didn't bother with it. I just wanted it to be over, and I deserved to go away, anyhow."

"Well, explain to me how it happened, then. Not the half-assed story that you gave to your defense team or the court, but the real deal. What went through your mind once you got to your mother's house?"

Zhao shimmies his bad hand further into his sleeve, once more.

"I went there angry when I shouldn't have. My real mistake was going there in the first place, but I did it anyway. It took about twenty minutes for me to walk there, and I was a mess the whole way over. I knocked on the door and when it opened, I saw her. She looked me dead in the eyes and said, 'I always figured you'd find me, one day'. But she didn't speak her words with joy or motherly love – she said it with resentment. She didn't get another word in after that, though, because before I knew it, I was just…on top of her. Strangling her with my good hand and beating her face in with my clubbed one. I don't remember much after that. I just lost control."

"That isn't at all what the papers reported on, or what was presented at court."

"I'm aware."

An older guard who's standing at the wall to my right catches my attention, signalling that my time's almost up.

Just like I did with Walter Gordon, I go in for the kill.

"Mr. Zhao, you said that you had no intention of killing your mother when you found her at her home. But you haven't said whether or not you had the intention of killing yourself, which was reported in your hospital discharge paperwork."

"No one's ever bothered to ask me about that bit before. I don't think anyone actually believed me when I said it."

He takes a few moments to speak again, stealing glances at his hand.

"When I found Grandma dead, I was distraught. I told you how devastated I was when I realized that she was gone and that I had nothing. Nothing left to live for. At that point, I'd made up my mind that I didn't want to live anymore, too. But I was also angry at my mother for everything, and so I went to confront her. I think I wanted closure of some kind before I did it. After I went there and – *killed* her," I note that Zhao struggles to say the word, "I went back home to do it. Police caught me when I was walking back, though. I wasn't exactly in my right mind, and I was walking slowly. I never got the chance to do it because they arrested me and put me away. I was hospitalized soon after, though. Apparently, I was a danger to others; I was hysterical."

"And are you glad?"

"That I lived? I suppose so. There's not much living to be done in prison, but it still counts as a life."

"No, I'm asking you if you're glad you killed your mother."

"I don't regret it, no."

After answering, Kassem looks at me with equal amounts of confusion and admiration, his head slightly tilted.

"Who are you, Sylvia St. James?"

I don't have time to answer because the guard has made his way over and is ushering me out of the visiting commons.

I don't know what I would have said, anyways. I don't know who I am.

I haven't known for seven years.

# **THEN**

June 10th, 1963
6:18 pm.

"Why are you here?" I ask him, speaking into his chest. He smells like the woods.

He finally releases me from his embrace and responds.

"I just wanted to come back and check on you. Is it so wrong for me to care?" He smiles.

"Well, everything's alright here." I pause,

then change the topic. "Did you come alone?"

"Yes, I did."

"Oh."

"And you know she wouldn't come here, even if we did leave together."

"Yeah, that's true."

She hates the farmhouse. It's been in his family for a few generations. They've never lived here full-time, simply because she dislikes it. So, he and I use this place as more of a cottage, a personal getaway. Somewhere we can come to escape. And where people like Sylvia *can't* escape. This place makes our escapades possible.

I love how the farmhouse smells like pine and dust despite it being relatively clean. The majority of the rooms aren't furnished, except the kitchen, living room, and dining room, but we've never needed anything more than that. A dark and dreary, near-empty basement is just fine for us. My favourite part about the farmhouse, though, is the property.

The house sits on an acre of land, undisturbed. Trees and thickets line the front, making the farmhouse difficult to see from the winding road leading to town. Gore Bay – no pun intended – is the closest town, but even that's a fair driving distance away.

I make a habit of maintaining the plants and flowers that grow in our garden. Especially the plots where the girls are buried. After dismembering each girl, he methodically places their individual body parts in a pre-dug hole in the back. Before I started helping, he would leave them be, just like that. But I decided to plant greenery and flowers over each grave to keep up the appearance of our well-manicured garden, even if no one is ever here to see it.

Far away from the body garden, we have a large pond. I used to think that our small body of water was as big as the ocean. I've always loved the water. We usually go swimming a few times every summer, but we haven't gone at all this past year. The dynamic between us is different, I think. I'm not sure if I like it or not.

I look out the kitchen window that faces the back of the farmhouse and admire the pond.

Then, he speaks.

"I should ask, though, why are you here? Why are you here, and not at home? Wait," he says, "how did you even get here without your own car? It's hours away from home."

So, so many questions. He must suspect something.

"After you left, I phoned up my Nan and got her to drive me over. She said that she didn't mind."

It's the truth, but I did lie about the pretenses when asking Nan for a ride.

"And I'm here to swim and bask in the sun. Why else would I be?"

He looks at me skeptically.

"You tell me."

"Look, I don't know what you're implying, but I don't like the accusation. I just wanted to get away from everything back home for a while."

"I'm not accusing you of anything, E."

"Now that you know everything's holding up here, are you going to get back to your weekend getaway?" I ask, playfully.

"You know, I'm hungry, and it's getting a bit late. I think I'll stay the night."

"Yeah, yeah, I agree. Of course."

Of course, he's staying.

Of course.

# THEN

June 10th, 1963
*7:00 pm.*

He's leaving now, driving into town to pick up some food so that he can make us a late dinner.

Once he realized that there was hardly anything in the fridge, he gave me a half hug and said he'd be back with food soon.

Something odd hangs in the air between us when he walks out the door. But the second he pulls out of the driveway, I immediately get to work. I swing the basement door open and barrel down the stairs, scaring Sylvia with my abruptness.

She flinches when I yank the duct tape off of her mouth.

"What's going on?" she asks.

I don't respond. I don't know what to tell her, so I don't tell her anything.

Sylvia is persistent, though, asking, "Who was that? The man upstairs."

"It was just a man. Upstairs."

I walk across the basement to retrieve the key to the handcuffs. The key is attached to a bracelet that I had hidden in the third drawer of an antique jewelry box. I crouch down on the floor to open the tiny drawer and grab the bracelet. I start coming toward Sylvia with such speed that she must think I've got a knife or something because she scurries backwards until she hits the wall and there isn't any farther back she can go.

She wouldn't be wrong in her assumption.

"Relax," I say.

Discretely palming the tiny bracelet and key, I show Sylvia my empty hands and her body relaxes. As I approach Sylvia, my senses are hyper-aware of the weight of the kitchen knife in my back pocket, blade up. I don't intend to use it if I don't have to. Not yet.

I walk past Sylvia's spot on the floor and head to the other side of the basement. In one swift motion, I grab the baseball bat leaning against the wall, lunge towards Sylvia, and bludgeon her head. Not enough to kill her, but enough to render her unconscious. Her body slumps to the ground and I kick her in the side, just to make sure she's not awake.

I consider unlocking the handcuffs that have adorned Sylvia's wrists but ultimately decide against it. He could come home any minute. It's better to wait until he's gone to bed.

Then I'll take care of her for good.

# NOW

March 27th, 1970
10:50 pm.

*Who am I?*

I haven't been able to stop asking myself this question since the interview with Kassem Zhao.

He asked me who I am rhetorically. A joke. But it's not a joke to me. I take myself seriously, maybe too seriously, but I have to be this way.

I lost myself seven years ago in that farmhouse, and I don't know who I am anymore.

I know who I've become but I don't know what I've become.

*Who am I?*
*What am I?*
Maybe I'm better off not knowing.

\*\*\*

My next interview is about a week away, and I don't know what to do with myself until then.

Up until now, my trips have been close together in proximity. The interviews with Gordon and Zhao were practically back-to-back.

I haven't had much time to myself since I first set out to do all of this, but that isn't necessarily a good thing. Not anymore. When I worked at the paper, I was grateful for the few hours a day that I had to myself. I was fine with not having friends, a partner, or family. I was happy enough with my own company and the occasional cuddles of Candy the cat, but things are different now. Things are changing.

After both interviews, I wrote down everything that I could remember about the questions I asked, as well as their answers. I made notes about their bodily cues and behaviour, and any defining characteristics that may give context to their psyches.

With so much time on my hands, I decide to read over the material from the interviews and try writing a rough draft of those chapters in the book.

Walter Gordon is a good introduction, I think. Gordon

is a domestic murderer; he's cryptic and un-remorseful but comes off as charming when he wishes. He displays some traits of psychopathy, which will undoubtedly demonize him to some extent.

The media didn't report on anything to do with Gordon himself. Not his job, his hobbies. It was as if he didn't exist as a person outside of his crime. But I'll spin it around, finally tell the story that he never got to.

Gordon wasn't born like this; he developed into the man he is today. He was a child and one who experienced traumatic familial circumstances, at that. This isn't public knowledge. Once I make the case for him, maybe then people will start to understand.

Kassem Zhao is an interesting case, too. He's young and uses sarcasm as some sort of defense mechanism. If what he says about killing his mother is true, if the murder truly wasn't premeditative, then the only other explanation is that he suffered a mental break. The death of his grandma would have been the catalyst that overloaded Zhao's brain with grief and anger. He would have lost himself in that grief. He also grew up knowing that his mother didn't want him because of his clubbed hand, and he was bullied for that same reason. That feeling of abandonment is enough to inflict some sort of emotional trauma on anyone.

Despite this, he was an honour roll student and helped his grandma out, whenever he could. He was a good kid and worked two jobs throughout secondary school.

I don't believe that Zhao is a cold-blooded killer. He could barely mutter the words *killed* or *murdered* because he was so ashamed of what he'd done. At the same time, he doesn't regret killing his mother, which makes for an interesting contradiction that I don't fully understand. This was never presented in court; he pleaded guilty, and that was that. I need to tell his story, too.

All of this reflecting on murder and the human mind has me thinking about what happened to me, all those years ago.

My thinking usually stops there, at that initial consideration of delving into my past. But not tonight. My mind isn't shutting off and I'm thinking too much about everything, and now I'm thinking about *it*.

About what happened.

My mind is jumbled everywhere and I'm thinking about how dark that basement was and how hot and sweaty we were and how the chains clinked on the concrete and how he came and ruined it all but also saved it all. I'm tired now and I want to sleep but I can't stop thinking. I wish I could stop my brain.

Why am I like this? Who am I? I return to the question again. And again:

*Who am I? Who am I? Who am I? Who am I?*

# B.C'S BLACK WIDOW: MURDERER ON THE RUN

—————— NOVEMBER 1969 ——————

Richmond police are searching for Darla Buchanan-Lyle, 24, who is suspected of killing three men.

All three victims had been married to Buchanan: Christopher Bartley, Raymond Hill, and Joseph "Joe" Lyle.

Buchanan skipped town after being invited to the police station for an interview regarding the untimely deaths of her husband and two ex-husbands. Investigators say there is no apparent motive at this time.

# NOW

April 2nd, 1970
*10:26 am.*

The mountain peaks are as sharp as knives.

I've never been to British Columbia before, or anywhere in Western Canada, for that matter, but I think I might want to vacation here eventually. Maybe once I sell this book and start making some real money. As it is, I struggle to buy myself the necessities and paying for the plane ticket from Toronto to Vancouver just about bankrupted me. The view more than makes up for it, though.

After landing at the airport, I rent a cheap car that I also can't afford, but the drive itself is like watching a film. The sky is clear, and crystal blue streams roll down and around the many mountains we pass on our way there.

When police were building a case on the Black Widow, she ran away, escaping into these mountains.

Well, not really.

She didn't make it very far. It turns out, you can't climb up the side of a snowy mountain in Mary-Jane strapped, leather shoes.

Her real name is Darla Buchanan-Lyle (née Hill, née Bartley). The papers dubbed her as the Black Widow, or, more specifically, B.C.'s Black Widow. Aptly named, given that she widowed herself by killing three of her husbands. It's a very creative moniker if you ask me.

Her first husband, an engineer named Christopher Bartley, 'fell' down the staircase and broke his neck.

Dr. Raymond Hill, her second husband, died from asphyxiation just one year later. Darla claimed that he slept with his head facing the pillow and had suffocated to death in his sleep.

Her third and last husband was a college professor by the name of Joe Lyle, and he died a more violent death than his predecessors.

In the cases of Christopher and Raymond, Darla was able to pass the deaths off as unfortunate accidents. But you can't accidentally stab someone in the chest half a dozen times, and that's what she claimed happened to Joe.

Darla first told police that she found Joe, already deceased, when she came home from the store. When police pressed her about it, she changed her story and said that she and Joe had gotten into an argument. She broke down crying and admitted Joe was physically violent towards her all the time, and things got out of hand on the night in question. Darla asserted that Joe began a verbal altercation that resulted in Darla killing her husband and acting in self-defense.

Anyone close to Joe Lyle testified that he was the kindest, most compassionate man that they knew. He quite literally couldn't hurt a fly and had a soft spot for animals. Darla was bullshitting the cops and Joe's family and friends, and people were starting to catch on.

That's when she made a run for it.

Once apprehended, Darla Buchanan-Lyle pleaded not guilty to two counts of third-degree and one count of first-degree murder, but the court ruled otherwise. The Black Widow was found guilty on all three charges and sentenced to life in prison. I remember reading about her case in the papers when it first happened a few years ago. It made headlines all the way in Ontario, travelling almost coast to coast.

I think that part of the reason why the country was so intrigued and disturbed by the Black Widow's murders is that she's a woman. Statistically, there are supposedly more male murderers than females; but that doesn't mean that we don't have the capacity to kill, or that we won't kill if given the means or motive. The Black Widow swapped the perpetrator-victim dynamic that dominates most of the crimes we hear about, and she captivated the nation in doing so.

Now, I'm sitting in front of her. Darla Buchanan-Lyle, the Black Widow.

"Hello, Darla," I say to her.

Darla resides at an all-women prison, and for some reason, the visiting rules appear to be laxer here. The visiting area is outside in a courtyard, where there is actual sunlight. The courtyard is enclosed by a gargantuan fence with barbed wire, but given the context, I suppose that it isn't a ridiculous precaution.

"What do you want?" asks Darla, and then spits on the ground. Lovely woman.

"I'm sure that someone already told you this, but-"

"No one told me anything."

"Okay, well, my name is Sylvia St. James. I'm a writer doing a piece on convicted criminals. Murderers, in particular."

"You've come to the right place. Welcome to paradise." Darla expressionlessly motions around to the courtyard, guards, and other inmates.

"Yes, it seems that I have."

I pause because I don't like her tone of voice at all,

and it's starting to bother me. There's no feeling, no distinction, whatsoever. At first, I thought she was just bitchy. But everything she says, she says in this way. The Black Widow is completely monotone and it's getting on my nerves.

"Do you get many visitors?" I ask.

"No."

"Do they let inmates in the courtyard often?"

"No."

"Are you enjoying your time out in the sun, then?"

"Yes."

I scribble observations in my notebook:

*Monotonous, seems like she could care less.*

Then, I add in, *Answers the bare minimum,* before contemplating my next move.

I need to figure out a way to elicit some sort of a reaction from her, or at the very least, a response more than a few words long.

"Darla, can you tell me a bit about yourself? What did you like to do, before all of this happened? Did you have any hobbies?"

"I'm an open book."

"Meaning?"

"Anything there is to know about me has been put out in the world already, one way or another."

"I know there was a lot of information out in the papers at the time of your capture, arrest, and trial, but I'm looking for something more personal. Are there any stories that stand out to you from your childhood or teenage years? Early adulthood? What about your marriages?"

"No. No. No. And no."

Her blank face and hollow tone are a little too eerie, even for me.

I lean closer to her and lower my voice. "You know, I'm on your side here."

"Are you, now?"

"I want to give you a chance to tell your side of the story. I want people to understand you, as a person. They don't have to agree with what you did or why you did it, but they do have to acknowledge that you're just like them. A person. And you know what a person has?"

I take a breath, surprising myself at how riled up I'm getting.

"Hobbies. Real people have a personality. Likes and dislikes. Interests. Quirks. The things that determine who you are. And if you don't have any of those things, well, I'm not sure that I can help you."

I get up in a huff, throwing my notepad into my purse and gathering my things. This isn't a bluff. I'm frustrated and have every intention of leaving right now. The other interviewees weren't nearly this difficult.

"Chess and violin. The colour red and pears; cats and spicy food. The human mind. My mouth twitches to the left sometimes regardless of whether I mean to do it or not."

I turn around and slowly put my things back down on the table.

"What?'

"I answered your questions. You're welcome."

I whip out my notepad again and write it all down. The way Darla recited those answers sounded robotic when paired with her monotonic vocal expression. Or, lack thereof. There was no hesitation or uncertainty in the recollection of my questions or her answers to them.

"You have a pretty good memory," I observe.

"I do, yes."

"Do you remember everything like that?"

"I remember what I remember."

An idea flashes through my mind, so I flip to a blank page in my notes and write down a list of numbers and letters.

*5 15 M 22 14 L Z V 103 N E 2001 J.*

The sequence is so random that I don't even remember half of what I just wrote when I tear off the sheet and slide it toward Darla. I try to be discreet about it since I suspect giving things to inmates is against the rules, no matter how small or harmless they are.

Darla slowly glances down at the paper with only her eyeballs. I snatch the sheet away after a few seconds, and she immediately begins repeating it.

"5 15 M 22 14 L Z V 103 N E 2001 J."

"So, you have a photographic memory or something of the sort."

"Nobody has ever told me anything like that, or put a label on it. But photographic memory does appear to fit the bill." She spits on the ground once more. "How nice of you to notice."

There is another inmate in the courtyard having visitation with her child and someone else, who I can only assume to be her own mother. The kid can't be more than five years old, and the woman accompanying him is now picking him up to leave. She says goodbye to the inmate and flips the boy over her shoulders so that he is facing behind her. He starts wailing and crying out for his mom, reaching for her as he's being carried away and throwing his fists through the air.

I remember feeling like that at the farmhouse.

"Why are you scowling?" Darla asks.

"I'm not scowling," I say, because I'm not. Or am I?

"Looks like I'm not the only one with issues, here."

"Everyone has issues. What's your point?"

"I have no point. It was just an observation."

"I'm the one making the observations here, not you."

"Whatever you say, Miss St. James."

A smile creeps across Darla's face that unsettles me so much that I actually feel a chill come over my body. I look down at my arms and see that the hairs are standing up straight; every last one.

# **THEN**

June 10th, 1963
7:38 pm.

It turns out that the only grocery store in Gore Bay closed at 5:00 pm., so he returned empty-handed.

He doesn't ask where all the food went, and I don't explain. We usually have a stash of snacks and perishable goods to fill the cupboards year-round, since he and I visit so frequently. Especially these past few years.

Tonight, though, all we had to eat was some cheddar cheese and saltine crackers, and cranberry juice. I hate cranberry juice.

Neither of us bothers to make conversation with each other, and instead, eat our lousy excuse of a dinner in peace. Only, I'm not at peace or in peace, and I don't think he is, either.

He's tense. His shoulders are stiff, his thick brows permanently furrowed, and his mouth is a fine, stiff line.

I'm naturally a quiet person and I always have been, so not making conversation isn't so out of the norm for me. He, however, is outgoing. A powerhouse. Charming. People flock to him and love to speak with him, even if it's just polite small talk. He's never this quiet, not even when we're at work with a girl. When we do that, he's subdued, but it's a different kind of silence. One of concentration, of savoury.

I finish my cheese and crackers, offering him the remainder of my cranberry juice. He refuses it with a shake of his head, so I dump it in the sink and listen as it gargles down the drain.

I can't go upstairs to bed. It's too early, and he might go snooping around in the basement if I go to bed before him. I think Sylvia is still knocked out right now, but I don't know how long she'll be asleep. I hope it's long enough for him to go to bed, and for me to transport her out of the basement.

"I'm pretty tired from the drive," he says.

He stands up from the kitchenette table and swipes the cracker crumbs from the tabletop onto the floor.

"I think I'll go up to sleep, now."

He doesn't wait for my reply, and instead, turns into the hallway and makes his way upstairs. It isn't even 8:00 pm., so there's no way he's this tired. Even if he's kind of old. That's how I know that he's lying.

But I'm lying, too.

It's just a matter of who's going to crack first; whose facade will fade away the fastest. And I'm determined that it won't be mine.

It can't be.

# NOW

April 2nd, 1970
10:49 am.

The time limit for my interview with the Black Widow is the longest yet, at 45 minutes long. But I've made up my mind that this interview is over.

I stand up and begin packing my things, for the second time.

"I hurt your feelings," states Darla. I don't respond. "Well, I'm not sorry."

The statement is so odd that I find *myself* responding.

"What did you say?"

"I said that I'm not sorry. If I hit a nerve, it's because

it needs to be hit. You're running away from something. I can tell."

I begin walking away from the Black Widow, this time, for good.

"And now you're running away from me."

She isn't raising her voice, despite me creating distance between us.

I reach the entrance to the main building and a guard walks me through the halls, and out of the courtyard. I clench my fists together the entire time.

When I get into my car, I slam the door and sit there for a while. I'm not angry, and I'm not frustrated like I was when she wasn't answering my questions. I don't know what I am. But I do know that I don't like the way these interviews are making me feel.

On the one hand, I'm excited and driven towards finishing this book; towards making a name for myself and making the paper regret ever firing me. On the other, I can feel myself unwinding with every passing day. I'm not sleeping, and I barely eat anymore. And I'm having bad thoughts, but I refuse to acknowledge them. I can't let myself do that or I'll fall into a rabbit hole that I won't be able to escape.

The thoughts continue to pour in anyways.

*I'm in the farmhouse, in the basement. It's summertime. It's hot outside, but there is cool air in the lower floor of the house. There is death lingering in the cool air, a presence that we can both feel. We are both down there. In the dark.*

I slam the gear shift forward, putting the car in drive, ignoring the scene and imagining myself running away from the thought.

The Black Widow is right, and she knows she's right. She knows that I know that she's right. She's an intelligent woman. As infuriating as that interview was, I do admire her high level of intelligence and envy her photographic memory.

I continue driving. I continue running away.

Run, run, run. All I do is run. I've been running for seven years.

*Will I ever stop running?*

# NOW

April 11th, 1970
*3:01 am.*

I'm shaking in my bed.

No, someone is shaking me. Or maybe I'm shaking myself. I awake panting and for a moment, I forget where I am.

I forget who I am.

"Hey, hey, you're alright," a voice says. "I got you."

I scurry backwards in bed at the sound of the voice.

"It's me, it's Damian. You had a nightmare or something. But you're alright now, I'm with you."

Oh.

I don't remember having Damian over last night, but I must have. And he must have stayed the night here, in my bed. I reach over to turn on my bedside lamp because I have an impulse to switch the lights on. When I hear the click of the lamp and see the light illuminate my bedroom, I relax.

But I don't see Damian.

I'm wide awake now but I rub my eyes with closed fists anyway. I open them again, and Damian still isn't there.

I turn off the lamp and go back to sleep.

# NOW

April 29th, 1970
*1:10 pm.*

I make sure to pack my tape recorder and notebook before leaving my apartment.

As I walk downstairs to meet Damian outside, I find myself questioning whether or not this is morally permissible. Probably not, but not many things in life are. People make poor decisions every day, and sometimes those decisions aren't really poor at all. They're a small sacrifice for the greater good, and that's how I'm choosing to view this meeting today.

I step outside in my most professional suede blazer and see Damian's Ford Pinto parked at the curb waiting for me. It's the colour of mud and possibly the ugliest car I've ever seen. You'd think he'd be able to afford something better with that fancy boss salary of his.

Damian greets me with a smile as I enter the car and sit down.

"So," he asks, "are you ready for today?"

"Are *you* ready for today?" I counter, playfully. "This is a big deal."

"Yeah, it is. I think I'm ready. As ready as I'll ever be, at least."

Damian begins the forty-five-minute drive to the facility where we'll be visiting his cousin, Lee.

"It looks like it's going to rain."

I look at the buildings as we drive by them, wondering about the people who live and work there. Apartments, storefronts, and office buildings, all in one condensed area. That's why I've always liked Toronto, especially the downtown core. It's easy to blend into the crowd when there are so many different people scattered throughout the city. You can be whoever you want, or you can even be no one at all. It's why I was so drawn here in the first place when I moved out.

"Sylvia?"

"Huh?"

"Where'd you go?" Damian chuckles, stealing a

glance at me. "You kind of checked out, there."

"Oh, sorry. I'm just tired."

"If you're not feeling good, I can turn around. We're not too far from your place."

"No!"

The vehicle jolts to the right at the abruptness of my voice, and then realigns itself.

"Sorry."

"It's alright. Look, I just want to tell you how much it means to me that you'll be here today. I know how stressed you've been with the book and the interviews, and I can see that you're exhausted, but I really appreciate it."

He lifts a hand from the steering wheel and squeezes my own hand, resting on my leg. He must think that my accepting his invitation to visit Lee with him is a romantic gesture.

"It's no problem," I say, smiling. "I'm feeling okay now, honestly."

We drive in silence as we exit the city radius, and it reminds me of when my dad and I would go on drives. Neither of us said anything to the other. We didn't need to. Along with the company of one another, the roar of the engine and swooshing of the breeze were always enough for us. Until it wasn't. Now he's gone, and there won't be any more drives.

For the first time in a long while – maybe, ever – I feel a sense of grief thinking about my father, about how he isn't here anymore. My mother has always struggled with her emotions when it comes to him. Right after it happened, she would cry herself to sleep, then wake up the next morning screaming and cursing into her pillow. Not me, though.

I've always had the skill of compartmentalizing feelings from facts. My brain is wired so that my emotions turn on and off, like a switch. It's convenient for situations like that when someone leaves or dies or does something bad. I can separate myself from it all with ease, which I'm grateful for.

"Sylvia?" Damian says, again.

"Yeah?"

"We're here. We've been here for a few minutes."

I focus on the scenery outside and realize that we're now in a parking lot.

"Shall we?"

I nod my head. Damian exits the vehicle and runs around to the passenger side to open up the door for me.

"What a gentleman," I say, sheepishly getting out of the passenger's side. When I slam the door shut and we begin walking away, I immediately turn back.

"I forgot my purse," I explain, over my shoulder.

And I'll definitely be needing my purse for this trip. Or, rather, what's inside of my purse. I retrieve my bag from the car, close the door, and sprint over to Damian.

"Let's do this."

# NOW

April 29th, 1970
2:03 pm.

Walking into the sterilized, white room, I'm drawn to the boy immediately.

There's a strange sort of contradiction here. His face is youthful, but there is a cold familiarity in his dark eyes; he has a melancholy presence to him.

From what Damian told me, I know that Lee Jenkins is seventeen years old and has been a ward of this institution for the past six years. This boy went from being caged and abused by his parents, to being locked away in a padded room where there aren't even any windows. It's a kind of cage in and of itself. At least he eats here, though, and gets some form of social interaction, albeit from his support staff.

The nurse who escorted us in brings two folding chairs out from the hallway and sets them down near Lee's hospital bed. She leaves the door half-open when she exits the room. I take my seat, but Damian remains standing. Lee is looking at him and doesn't break eye contact as he sits up from his bed.

Damian takes a wary step forward.

"I don't know if you remember me, but I'm your cousin, Damian."

Lee must remember because tears are forming in his eyes. The two mutually travel in each other's direction and meet in the middle with a hug. The nurse watching from the doorway looks weary of the physical contact but leaves them be. After a minute, Damian releases himself from the hug and Lee follows suit, but I can see that he's sad to end the embrace.

Damian moves his chair closer to the bed, and I take this opportunity to peek into my purse and turn on the tape recorder. I hit the record button, close the purse flap, and bring my seat closer, too.

Everyone is quiet. I don't think anyone knows what to say, so I introduce myself.

"Hi, Lee. My name is Sylvia. I'm Damian's friend."

He looks in my direction but doesn't speak. Lee then

turns his focus to Damian.

"I missed you," Lee says.

"I missed you, too. I was really upset to hear about everything that happened to you. It's a really screwed up way to live, and an even worse way to grow up."

"I'm still growing up."

"You're right, and this isn't a very good place to grow up in, either," I chime in.

"Guess so. Still better, though."

We're silent again.

I didn't think that it would be this awkward. I study Lee's face. He's expressionless and his eyes are dark, but he doesn't look inherently evil. He's not a monster. I think that out of all the interviews, this might be the deal-breaker for the reader; the one case that makes them think.

If a child grew up in the conditions Lee grew up in, and then killed his parents, his abusers, would that child be a monster? Would you place the blame fully on them? It's a moral dilemma, and one that I hope to capitalize on. The answer is no. Blame can fall on both the child and the parents; it's not an *either-or* situation. Things in this world aren't always black and white, which is what I'm looking to illuminate in this book, through the context of killers.

"What was it like?" I blurt out.

Damian gives me a disapproving look and shakes his head subtly, but I continue.

"Growing up with parents who abused you and neglected you. Living in filth and hunger. What was that like, Lee?"

Lee begins to cry, and Damian leans forward to comfort him. It strikes me that Lee is still an eleven-year-old boy in almost every way.

Lee speaks with a simple vocabulary and has trouble maintaining eye contact. He hardly knows how to function in a social situation such as this one. Outside of having an almost-adult body, Lee's mind and emotions are practically stunted from what he's been through.

"Hell," Lee finally murmurs.

Damian rubs Lee's shoulder, but Lee shrugs him off. Damian takes the hint and returns to his regular seating position.

"It was hell. Living hell. Hell, hell, hell."

He's crying more, now, and Damian stands up to find the nurse from the hall, who must have left for a bathroom break, or something.

As he's walking away, I ask Lee, "Why did you do it? What made you snap?"

Lee is bawling now, rocking and dry heaving in between his sobs.

Having found the nurse, Damian rushes in with her, followed by a team of other nurses. I stand up and move closer to Lee, trying to get an answer before I'm inevitably forced to leave. Damian stares at me from a few feet away, his eyes fuming, so I cease my efforts and make my way out of the room.

I'm almost out the door when Lee finally responds to my question.

"I did it," Lee says, raising his voice, "because it couldn't get any worse. There isn't anything below rock bottom."

One of the nurses sedates Lee with a long syringe, and as Damian and I exit the room, his cries become quieter and then stop, altogether. Damian and I are silent until we're outside of the building, making our way to his car.

I fumble getting inside the passenger's seat and drop my purse onto the car floor, all my belongings pouring out. My tape recorder falls out, too, and I can't get it back into my purse in time. Damian sees it, and then he loses his shit.

"What the hell do you think you're doing with that?" I don't respond. "I was angry enough that you egged him on the way that you did in there, but this? You went behind my back. I trusted you to come and support me, but instead, you betrayed me. Whatever it is that we have going on here, ends right now. Get out. Get out of my car."

I'm genuinely surprised at how upset Damian is. I've never seen him even remotely like this before. Damian has always been so cool and composed, kind and considerate.

I stay sitting in the car seat and say, "There was never

anything between us for you to end."

"Get. Out. Of. My. Car," he growls.

This time, I oblige. Damian drives away immediately, almost leaving skid marks in the parking lot.

I examine my tape recorder to make sure it's not damaged or broken. Most importantly, to make sure that I was recording that meeting with Lee. What he said there at the end was important.

When I see that everything's fine, I begin the long walk home so that I can finish up my manuscript.

# NOW

*May 10th, 1970*
*11:00 am.*

I knock on my mother's front door; this is the first time I've left the house in a long while.

She's completely moved out of the old house, *our* old house, and I'm dismayed to see that her new abode is a five-minute drive from my own.

My first impression is that the front yard looks like a piece of shit, as if the previous owners never mowed the lawn, plucked a weed, or planted a flower. The house itself is a modest bungalow. From the exterior, it looks dated and mundane. It's definitely a downgrade from our old house.

"I'm around back!"

I follow the sound of my mother's voice around the side of the house, where she's kneeling in the dirt, surrounded by freshly planted flowers and shrubs. She finishes scooping some dirt with a gardening shovel and stabs the tool into the soil as she arises.

"I would hug you, but I'm all dirty," she says, with a chuckle. Not that I'm complaining.

My mother leads me through a fence door where I see a further abyss of weeds in the backyard. It smells like animal shit.

"Holy," I say. "Who lived here before you?"

For once, I'm in a good mood. I'm joking and being sarcastic, and I think the change takes her by surprise. It's for a good reason, too.

My mother hides a tight smile and shrugs her shoulders to be nonchalant.

"It was cheap, and that's all that matters to me. More cash to fund my retirement," says Mom, with a wink.

Mom takes off her gardening gloves and throws them on the rotted wood of the deck, and then proceeds to lead me into the house.

The interior of the place is barren. No photographs or artwork are displayed on the walls, and there isn't a single piece of furniture other than the couch and dining room table.

"I actually couldn't bring myself to take most of the things we packed along. His things. So many items have memories latched onto them like leeches. I want to look at a piece of art that I love without thinking about how your father bought it for me as a seventh-anniversary present. And when I look at a family photo, I don't want to be reminded of the fact that you'd broken the frame in half during a tantrum. This home is a new beginning for me. A blank slate. I figured I would start off on the right foot."

She smiles at me and tells me to take a seat.

"I actually had something that I wanted to show you," I tell her, optimistically.

"Oh? And what's that?"

I dig into my purse and pull out the thick paper manuscript that is my book, placing it in her hands.

"Could you grab me my reading glasses, please? My eyes are getting bad, these days."

I do as she asks and then return to my seat. Her face is one of confusion and repulsion. At least, that's what it looks like from here.

"I wrote a book," I explain.

"I can see that, yes."

She continues flipping through the pages, her eyes skimming over the text I've worked so tirelessly on. It's like a slap in the face.

"You aren't even reading it."

"Where on earth did you come up with these characters? This idea? It's... sick."

"They're not characters. They're real people who committed real crimes, and I interviewed them all, first-hand."

"You did *what*?" I cross my arms in child-like defiance. "Do you know how dangerous that is? You could have been killed!"

"Inside high-security prison units with officers and guards breathing down your neck? Oh, yes. It's so very life-threatening."

"How does the paper feel about your... project?"

"I got laid off from the paper, and I'm better off on my own."

I scoff when she hands me back the manuscript, abruptly shoving it into my grasp as if it were on fire. I get off the couch and talk down to her, giving her a piece of my mind.

"I've been working on this for months. I've been slaving over the typewriter, writing this, *for months*. I've had this idea in my mind for almost a year. And you have the audacity to call me sick? Fuck you. Fuck you and this sorry excuse of a family."

She doesn't bother responding and lets me leave her new house with ease.

I slam the door on the way out and immediately make my way to the side of the house, where all her garden work is. I pluck the shovel from the dirt and stab at her newly planted gardenias until there isn't a single flower left intact.

The petals lay scattered on the ground like drops of blood when I step on them to leave.

# NOW

May 11th, 1970
*11:56 pm.*

Something is missing, there must be.

I've been sitting around all day trying to figure out what it is.

My mother reacted so poorly to the manuscript that there must have been something setting her off. Maybe she didn't like my interview with Lee. In the book, I refer to him as the U.A.C., or underage child. I legally can't use his name in relation to the case and what he did to his parents, but I sure as hell can change his identity. Besides, Mom never even got that far in. I arranged the book so that Lee's section is the second-last, and she stopped reading – skimming – after Walter Gordon, who is in the first section. She didn't even give it a chance.

Is it my writing? No, I worked at a newspaper, for God's sake. I know I can write well, and so does she. Maybe there *is* something missing, then. A piece of the puzzle not yet discovered; the puzzle being an amalgamation of the criminal psyche.

Today, I had only a piece of toast for breakfast. I'm starving but I won't allow myself anything else until I figure out what's wrong with my book. I haven't slept in over twenty-four hours, either, and I won't start now. Regardless of how drained I am, I won't rest.

Not when there's work to be done.

\*\*\*

It's him. It's him!

At 4:00 am., I crack the code.

I don't know why I didn't think of this before, why it wasn't a component of my plan in the first place. This is it, the last piece I need to truly sensationalize this text. And now, I can finally allow myself some rest.

When I wake up tomorrow morning, I'm going to visit Victor Cobb in prison.

# THEN

June 10th, 1963
*10:00 pm.*

I watch the grandfather clock in the family room hit 10:00 pm. and listen as the chimes ding ten times.

It's eerily quiet after the chimes subside. I've been sitting on the couch for the past few hours, waiting in silence. He hasn't moved around once upstairs, not even to go to the washroom. Or, if he has, I haven't heard him. That's what worries me.

The floorboards are old, though. They creak, everywhere in the house.

I would have heard him if he'd gotten up, wouldn't I?

# THEN

June 11th, 1963
*12:09 am.*

He should definitely be asleep by now. He has to be.

I've never seen him stay up past midnight, and I hope this isn't the occasion where he finally decides to do it.

I get up from the couch, leaving a sunken impression on the cushion from where I sat for almost three hours straight, staring at the ceiling. I tiptoe across the floor, trying to avoid the creaking of the wooden boards; the same noises I so desperately listened for earlier.

I open the door to the basement, looking around the main floor for any signs of activity. There's nothing. I creep down the steps and I can barely see in the pitch black. When I get to the bottom of the stairs, I pull the string attached to the small light fixture on the ceiling, and a dull luminescence fills the immediate area.

Sylvia is still passed out on the concrete, in the same position she was in when I left her, hours earlier.

I take the bracelet with the key out of my pocket and unlock Sylvia's handcuffs from the metal pipe on the wall. Her wrists have ligature marks on them from how tight I had the restraints.

That must have been uncomfortable.

I place the cuffs on the ground and grab hold of Sylvia's hands. There's no way I'm getting her up the stairs, period, let alone quietly. I'm not strong enough to do it on my own. I start dragging her towards the cellar door that leads to the backyard. It's what we use when we're moving body parts from the basement to the garden to be buried. Sylvia isn't wearing any shoes, so I manage to move her without any scraping sounds. I drop her body to the floor, freeing my hands so that I can open the cellar door.

It makes a noise so loud that I jump.

I have to get this done, *now*.

I pick up her arms again and drag her outside, leaving the door open behind me. It's the middle of the night and there isn't any light other than the moon and –

God damn it.

The light in his bedroom is on. I can see it through the window.

I continue dragging Sylvia up the slant from the cellar door to the backyard, and it's exhausting having to move her uphill. I don't stop, though. I keep moving forward, forward, until I'm across the lawn and in front of the pond. I didn't really know what I was going to do about Sylvia until now, my body had made up my mind for me.

I carefully slide Sylvia's body into the water. Once she's fully submerged, I lean over the bank and hold her head down. She doesn't fight back because she's still unconscious.

After a minute, I step back from the edge and examine Sylvia's limp body, floating upwards in the water. She'd sink to the bottom, soon. Her life would be erased from existence as if she'd never been here at all.

Looking over my shoulder, I see that the light in his room is now shut off. He must have gone back to bed.

I've done it, I made it through my first time! After such a close call with him coming home early, I contemplate whether or not I'll ever try this by myself again.

I hear a splash, and I don't have time to finish the thought. It leaves my brain as quickly as my feet leave the grass underneath them. Something grips my ankles and pulls me backward.

I hear another splash and realize with a gasping breath of water that it's me, being pulled under.

# NOW

May 12th, 1970
*10:49 am.*

I'm in the waiting room of yet another prison, right outside of Toronto.

The guards give me wary looks as they lead me into a more secure area of the grounds, and into the visitation room. They know who I'm here to see. I hear the door behind me, and I'm alone in this metal box of a room. The visitation commons here are composed of individual rooms where inmates can meet their families in private. It's not actually private, though, since a guard watches the encounter through a square window. But I'm glad that we can talk by ourselves, one-on-one, without anyone overhearing the conversation. That would be sure to ruin everything.

I wait for at least another ten minutes before he arrives. I hear the clank of his ankle chains and handcuffs before I see him, the restraints similar to the ones he adorned his hostages with. He takes his seat across from me and the guard who brought him in leaves us be.

I lean onto the cheap, metal table and close my hands together, making eye contact for the first time in over seven years.

"Hi, Dad."

# THEN

June 11th, 1963
*12:13 am.*

My arms and legs flail instinctively under the water, thrashing outwards.

There's a pressure on my head pushing me down and I open my eyes, which subsequently burn from being underwater. Everything is dark and blurry, but I can just make out the figure of someone above me. That someone is Sylvia. She's in the water, too, but Sylvia is using me like a buoy to stay afloat whilst simultaneously keeping me submerged. I'm running out of air, and against my will, my mouth opens, gasping for oxygen. Water pours into my lungs instead, burning my insides.

There are rocks scattered on the floor of the lake, and so I make a move for one. I stop fighting back against Sylvia, letting her think she's successfully pushed me down. I swim another foot or so until I'm at the bottom and grab a hold of the largest rock that I can manage. I swim up to the surface, the rock heavy in my grip, until I see Sylvia's legs.

Our struggle had taken us to the middle of the lake, and she's now swimming back to dry land. I feel like I'm going to pass out from the lack of air in my body, so I make my move. I swim upwards and emerge from the water, gasping for air and slamming the rock against the back of Sylvia's head. After the impact, I drop the boulder with a splash and paddle closer so that I'm facing her.

Sylvia slowly sinks into the water, but I'm not done with her yet. I violently hoist her back up and look at her. She's still conscious, but her face is blank. Sylvia's glossy blue eyes contrast the darkness around us.

Sylvia looks as if she wants to say something or ask me something.

Perhaps, "Why?" or "How can you live with yourself?" or something of the sort.

I don't allow her the chance to ask any questions. I put my hands around Sylvia's neck and squeeze.

I wring her neck like a water-soaked towel, capitalizing on a strength I didn't know I was capable of; but now that I do know, I plan on using it. I keep squeezing and squeezing until those glossy doe eyes lose the life inside of them, and until I feel her body go limp in my clutch.

I keep on strangling her until the pain in my hands and fingers wake me from whatever reverie I was just in.

I release Sylvia and watch as her body sinks into the lake.

## THEN

June 11th, 1963
2:31 am.

I'm still in my soaking wet clothes when I get into bed and go to sleep.

I don't remember how I got here. All I know is, that for the first time since all of this began, I can relax.

# THE MAN

*At 8:30 am., the man wakes up and senses, again, that something is wrong; but this time, he is at the house.*

*There is a trail of small puddles beginning at the door to the basement and leading across the floor, and up the stairs.*

*It could just be spilled water, or maybe even a leak. But the man knows better. He opens the door and walks down the stairs. In the corner of the basement, he sees his fold-out chairs and table. The man always keeps the girls he takes in this corner. His pair of handcuffs are sprawled on the concrete, attached to the metal pipe, lining the walls.*

*This is his set-up.*

*Only, it is not.*

*The man had no part in this, and he knows now that his suspicions were correct. Then, the man realizes something terrifying.*

*Who was in these cuffs? And where are they, now?*

*If she had already killed whoever it was and disposed of the body, they could be in big trouble. To the man's knowledge, she has never done this on her own before. The man wishes she had never helped him with the previous girls in the first place, but he had no other choice than to let her participate. She would have ratted him out.*

*Though, maybe that would have been the better alternative. The man also could have killed her, right then and there, but he would likely be in jail if he had done that.*

*The man has made a monster.*

\*\*\*

*The cellar door has been left partially open, and as the man steps into the backyard, he fears the worst.*

*If the water puddle and cellar door are any indicators of how organized this operation is, there is going to be a big mess for the man to clean up.*

*First, the man looks in the garden for any uprooted dirt and digging sites. The topiary and soil are undisturbed. The man is not sure whether or not that is a good thing. Next, he looks in the garbage containers at the side of the property, but there is nothing there, either.*

*Maybe the man is wrong. Maybe she had just gone for a late-night swim and was too tired to clean the puddles or shut the cellar door all the way.*

*The man continues looking around the plot.*

*Across the way, on the other side of the pond, he sees*

*something. A body. The man hesitantly approaches the figure, which is laying near the oak tree at the rear of their lake.*

*The trunk of the old oak tree is covered with smears of crimson. Blood. The body, a young girl, by the looks of it, lays next to it on the grass.*

*The girl is facing the ground, but the man can see that the right side of her skull is cracked open. The right half of her face has been rendered unrecognizable. Pieces of skin have been removed from her face entirely, revealing the connective tissue beneath. Even though the man could only see that half of the girl's face, he is positively appalled at the extent of the violence.*

She looks like Dr. Jekyll and Mr. Hyde, *the man thinks.*

*The right portion of the girl's face is something straight from a horror film. The whole scene is.*

*The man does not touch the body, nor does he touch the tree. He keeps his distance and refrains from physically interacting with the crime scene because that is what this is. A crime scene. The man has been the perpetrator of many crime scenes before, yes, but none as messy as this. He needs to take extra caution.*

*His kills are clean and organized. Methodical. His disposals are equally as deliberate. After dismembering his victims' limbs on a large tarp in the basement, the man buries them in a pre-dug grave near the shrubs or flowers on their property. Then they plant more shrubs or flowers on top of the dirt when the body has been disposed of.*

*The man has not been caught so far; not by the police, at least. She had caught him by a fluke, and now everything he has done is in jeopardy.*

She could not have done this, *the man thought.* It is too gruesome, too graphic.

*But she did do it, and she left a mess behind her.*

*A mess that could take them both down.*

# NOW

May 12th, 1970
11:05 am.

"Evie, what a surprise."

Hearing him say my name, my real name, has me taken aback. I'm not sure why. I feel the need to clarify.

"Actually," I explain, "I don't go by Evie anymore."

"Then, what name do you go by?"

I clear my throat even though I don't need to.

"My name is Sylvia St. James."

"No, it's not."

"My name is whatever I want it to be. And it's been Sylvia since my eighteenth birthday when I moved out."

I remove my hands from the tabletop and place them on my lap.

He doesn't respond immediately, and I take this moment to look at him. Really, really look at him.

I remember him as being a well-to-do guy with a regular office job and a regular family. With one exception, of course. The last time I saw him, he had dark brown hair styled in a comb-over. His face was absent of any wrinkles or imperfections, and he always sported a smile wherever he went.

In my memory, I preserved him as a mannequin; an idea of a person frozen in time. The man sitting in front of me is practically a stranger.

His hair is dishevelled, wavy streaks of gray sticking out in every direction. Wrinkles decorate the slack skin on his face and neck, stubble spotted around his jaw.

"You know, Evie, that's disappointing to hear. I'm assuming your mother doesn't know about this little change?"

"My name is Sylvia."

My face is getting hot.

"You stole that name."

I take a breath and decide to start on my questions. I pull out my notebook, where I've written some prompts down.

"I'm sure you're wondering why I'm here," I begin. "Well, I'm writing a book. A piece highlighting the minds and psychological make-ups of killers. I have the manuscript completed but it's missing something. Someone. That's where you come in."

"Oh, goody."

He smiles jovially and leans forward, placing his chin in his hands and his elbows on the table. Through the little window, I see a guard flinch from the sudden movement.

"Is it me? Am I who you're missing?"

His expression changes like a bolt of lightning, and he's now wearing a straight face, his eyes piercing mine.

"In that case, you don't need to ask me anything. You know all you need to know, and more."

"Give me a refresher."

I pause to look down at my sheet, the questions more direct than the ones I asked other interviewees.

"Tell me their names. Victor Alexander Cobb, please recount to me the name of every girl you were convicted of kidnapping and murdering."

"Dramatic, dramatic. You always were one for drama."

He pauses and strokes his chin in fictitious thought.

"Their names. Ah, yes. What were they, now? June Courtley. Barbara Fitzpatrick. Sasha Zimmerman. Bess Boynton. Laurel Anders. Rita da Silva."

"You're missing one."

"You said *convicted*. And besides, that one was all you, my dear."

I ignore him.

"Which was your favourite?"

"The first one, June."

I didn't expect him to actually answer, let alone, answer without hesitation. That question wasn't even on my sheet, it was improvised. Now, I'm glad that I asked it. I move down the list of questions, daring myself to be blunter and more impulsive.

"Why are you like this? Did anything traumatizing happen to you during your childhood?"

"No, nothing like that."

"Any familial history of mental illnesses?"

"Not that I know of."

"Let's go in a new direction, then. Why start in your late thirties? Why begin your killings during what's meant to be the best days of your life? You had a loving wife, a daughter, a nice house, and a steady job. So, why?"

I slap my hands down on the table for emphasis. It's a question I've wanted to know for years. In all the time we spent together, he never once told me why. I just went along with it because he made me.

"I'll take a pass on that one."

"No, you won't. This is my interview and I call the shots."

I straighten myself in the chair and try to look more intimidating.

"Why?"

He doesn't speak, doesn't breathe.

"Victor, answer the question."

"Whatever happened to good old Dad?"

"You lost the right to that title when you started killing innocent girls."

"You've got to be kidding me. No, seriously. If you're not joking right now, then you really need to take a look in the mirror, *Evie.*"

His cuffed hands resting on the table begin to squirm within the restraints.

"I don't know what you're talking about. Now, if we could just get back to the question."

"I'll answer your God-damned question if you own up to what you did." I look around the room, peaking at the guards through the window. "Relax, they can't hear us. You can confess to murder and walk right out that door, through the gates, and waltz back into your life with no consequences. I've already taken the fall for everything you ever participated in."

"Okay, I'll admit it if you tell me everything. Brutal honesty about why you did what you did, and your consent to use this information in my book."

"Deal."

"Out with it, then. Why did you start killing when you did? What made you snap?"

"Nothing made me snap; it was a decision I made. A decision to start killing to avoid me actually snapping, and in a much worse way. You'd always been a shitty kid. Temper tantrums all the time, punching and scratching your mother, doing the opposite of whatever we told you to do just to spite us. But you were young and innocent, and we figured it was a phase. When you hit puberty, your behaviour only got worse. Maybe not in your actions, but my tolerance of them. You had just turned fourteen when it first happened. I got this feeling of boiling anger when I looked at you."

I raise my eyebrows at this. I never acted this way.

"You were growing into a young woman and were no longer this little girl whom I gave the benefit of the doubt to. You didn't grow out of your fits; you grew into them. And I grew to dislike you for it. One night, it was just us at home. Your mother was visiting a friend out of town, and it stormed, so she stayed overnight. When I went to check on you in the evening, you weren't in your bed. You had sneaked out somewhere. I was pissed off that you left without telling me and hoped that you would freeze to death. And I'm not exaggerating. That's when I knew I had a problem. I stayed up the entire night until you got home at three o'clock in the morning. I heard you sneak in through your bedroom window, I heard the bumps and noises. A few hours later I went into your room and just about strangled you in your sleep. I knew I couldn't go on like this. I was going to kill you, and as much as I hated you, there was a part of me that still loved you and hoped you'd grow out of the behaviour. A part of me that thought I'd get my little girl back. Weeks passed, but nothing changed. Your fits turned into screaming matches and your small acts of defiance became acts of violence. And me? My restraint to act on it was weakening every day.

When I was out of town on a business trip, it just sort of happened. It was pouring rain and I was driving back to my hotel when I saw a girl who looked just like you, walking and drenched. I pulled the car over and asked her if she wanted a drive home, and she accepted. She told me her name was June and that she was sixteen. She took dance classes and her birthday was coming up the next week. I couldn't get over how much she looked like you. The physical similarities were so pronounced, that it could have been you in a few years. The same shade of blonde hair, same blue-grey eyes. I was just going to drive her home, but once I made the connection, I couldn't control myself.

I pulled the car over onto a quiet road, turned the ignition off, and strangled her until her skin matched the colour of her eyes. But I wasn't strangling *her*. I was imagining it was you the entire time. She became this substitute without me even realizing it. The next few girls didn't look like you, but they were around the same height and age. They were an outlet so that I didn't harm you. I didn't particularly enjoy doing it, but I enjoyed that it kept me from ruining my family.

Two years and six murders later, I turned myself in after your stunt with Sylvia. That nonsense had gone on long enough and I wanted to protect you from the fallout in case the cops ever put anything together on their own. So, after I cleaned up your mess at the farmhouse, I drove myself to the police station in town. I surrendered myself and said I acted alone. That way, you would never be connected to the crimes. Believe it or not, I did it all because I loved you. I did it for you."

# NOW

May 12th, 1970
11:23 am.

For a moment, I'm speechless.

I scribble some notes and ask my next question.

"Why include me, then? Why force your daughter, who you apparently cared *so much* for, into being your accomplice?"

I fidget with a cheap ring on my index finger, awaiting his response.

"Evie, are you joking?"

"This is no joking matter."

"I only agreed to be candid if you would own up to what you did."

"Okay, then. I admit that you threatened me and made me into your criminal accomplice. Me, who was a young, impressionable teenager. Me, your helpless daughter. I admit that I helped you kill those innocent girls because you threatened that it would be me, otherwise. I admit that you are the world's worst father and have traumatized me for the rest of my life. And I'm glad you're rotting in jail, where you belong."

He sits back in his seat and laughs, the handcuff chains clinking in sync with his cackles. He pops up out of his chair and begins yelling, shocking me.

"*You* walked in on me, remember? *You* threatened that if *I* didn't let you join in, then you'd rat me out to the police. It was *you* who voluntarily lured the girls, not because I made you, but because you enjoyed it. Admit it. Admit that you enjoyed the part you played. Admit that you wanted more than that part, and so you went behind my back and took her. Killed her."

I look outside the small window to see that the guard watching us has now left. I remain facing my father but let the peripherals of my eyes scan the room to make an exit plan, if necessary.

"I don't know what you're talking about."

"You know exactly what I'm talking about. I took the fall for you. I cleaned up your mess for you. I did all of this for you, and you can't even give me back an ounce of honesty. But that's my fault for traumatizing you, right? Because I'm such an awful parent?" When I don't answer, he repeats himself.

"*Right?*" he roars.

"Right."

There might as well be steam blowing out of my ears, but I take a deep breath and stand up to leave. I gather my things and head towards the door without saying a word — but I'm yanked backwards before I reach the exit. I whip my head around, daggers in my eyes, and try to unlatch my hand from his limited grasp. He's too strong.

"Let go of me. Right now," I demand.

"No, Evie, listen. I'm sorry, okay? I didn't mean to upset you. Please stay and talk with me. I haven't seen you in years and I want to make things right between us. I just got angry before. I get like that all the time. Happy, angry, happy, angry. It's like my emotions are on a see-saw, up and down."

He pulls me closer, as he stumbles over his words.

"If you want to believe that that's what happened then I won't stop you. It's not like anyone would know either way. Just, please stay with me, Evie."

His eyes are pleading, and as I look at his pathetic face, a sense of calm falls over me like a blanket.

I quiet my voice to an indignant hush. "My name isn't Evie Cobb. My name is Sylvia St. James. And you,

Victor, aren't my father. You aren't anyone at all. Do you expect me to feel pity for you? Because all I feel is indifference. I couldn't care less what happens to you, or *Evie*, for that matter. Evie is dead. She doesn't exist. You don't have a daughter anymore."

I capitalize on his momentary shock, thrashing my arm away from him. Once I'm free from his touch, I look out the window to see the guard returning, and I get an idea. In one swift motion, I dig my nails into my cheek and drag them down, down, until I smell rust.

My father stares back at me, confused. I look him dead in the eyes and screech so loudly, in a voice so unfamiliar, that it even surprises me. The guard comes running in, as I stumble backwards against the wall, pointing my finger.

"He, he-he assaulted me," I whisper, just quiet enough to signal shock but loud enough for the guard to hear.

The guard rushes over to me, yelling into his walkie for backup. I nod my head ever so slightly as I'm helped to my feet and guided out of the room. I don't bother looking back at my father because I already know the pathetic, hurt expression that would be plastered on his face.

Instead, I internally relish in the punishment he'll undoubtedly receive for attacking a visitor and take comfort in knowing I've won.

# THEN

June 11th, 1963
*10:43 am.*

"I know what happened, but I don't know how it happened."

My father looks at me with a look I've never seen before. It's not quite rage, but it's not quite fear, either. It's one of dread, of anticipation.

"How can you not know what happened?" he retorts. "You killed someone! That's not something you can easily forget."

"She tried to kill me, so I killed her. That's that."

It's not a lie. I do remember Sylvia dragging me under after I left her in the lake for dead. She tried to kill me, and in return, I killed her. I hit her with a rock and choked her until she'd taken her last breath. After that, though, I don't remember what happened.

When he'd taken me out back to show me what I'd done, I almost couldn't believe it. I had created a piece of art.

I'd painted her blood on strands of grass and smeared it across the great oak tree. Sylvia's neck twisted at an abstract angle, revealing half of her mangled face. I don't remember losing myself like that. I don't remember doing this.

But I wish that I did.

# THEN

June 11th, 1963
*11:05 am.*

He's gone into town.

I helped him to move Sylvia's body from the backyard into the basement. When he began gathering supplies to start the cleaning process, he cussed and told me that we were out of cleaner. Apparently, the cleaner we regularly use for the aftermath is some special, industrial-grade cleaner. He needed to go buy more of it, and it just *has* to be this particular kind.

Part of me wishes that we didn't have to clean it all up. Looking at that scene made me proud. I was a survivor. I had overcome Sylvia in a physical altercation when she attacked me. I had never been in a fight before. The adrenaline that ran through my blood was a euphoria, unlike anything I'd ever experienced before.

He doesn't see it that way, though. He says that I was sloppy and irresponsible for doing this without him.

He says that "this little stunt" could get us both in big, big trouble.

I say, bring it on.

# THE MAN

*The man parks his truck and exits the vehicle. He is calm and waves to other townsfolk as he walks down the street and into the hardware store.*

*Calm.*

*He has to remain calm. Normal.*

*The man has never experienced this level of panic before. Not with any of the previous girls, not with anything.*

This cannot go on any longer, *he thinks.*

*Once the man is inside, he pretends to browse around, looking at products that he has no intention of purchasing. The store owner sees this and approaches him.*

"Hey, Victor," the owner says.

"Hi there, Paul."

"What brings you in today?"

"Just picking up some things. Doing some construction on the old farmhouse."

"Anything that I can help you with?"

"No."

*The man realizes that he responded too intensely. He can see it in the owner's face.*

"Alrighty, well, let me know if I can be of any assistance to you, Vic."

*The man nods in the owner's direction. The man and the owner typically converse whenever they meet in town. The owner is a very personable fellow. The man feels a morsel of guilt over this but sweeps the thoughts out of his mind.*

*He makes his way up and down the aisles. The man*

*grabs paint thinner, a small bucket of dark cherry paint, wood stain, and of course, his special cleaner. He only needs the cleaner, but he does not want to come off as suspicious.*

*The man buys everything and leaves without another word.*

\*\*\*

*The man is driving back to the farmhouse.*

*As he approaches the edge of town, he sees something that catches his eye. It is a piece of paper, stapled to a telephone pole at the side of the road. The man pulls over and gets out of his truck so that he can read it.*

# The Daily

Issue 020                                              June, 1963

## Local teen gone missing

The parents of sixteen year-old Sylvia St. James are appealing to the public to help find their daughter. After going out with a friend on June 9th, 1963, Miss. St. James never returned home. The friend Miss. St. James visited has not yet been identified.

## HAVE YOU SEEN THIS PERSON?

FULL NAME: Sylvia Marie St. James
DOB: May 5, 1947
AGE: Sixteen
SEX: F
HEIGHT: Five feet, three inches
WEIGHT: 115 lbs
MISSING SINCE: June 9, 1963
IDENTIFYING CHARACTERISTICS: Brown hair, blue eyes, leaf-shaped birthmark on left arm

# THE MAN

*The man begins to panic.*

*This cannot be happening. This never happened with any of the other girls. They had always picked up the girls in a different town or hamlet and brought them back to the farmhouse. There had never been any missing person posters in and around the main town.*

*Calm.*

*The man has to stay calm.*

*Calm.*

*The man has to stay calm.*

*The man cannot stay calm.*

*The man goes into his truck and screams until he has no voice.*

*Then he drives home to clean up his daughter's mess.*

# **THEN**

June 11th, 1963
3:29 pm.

He isn't home yet.

It's been hours and my father still hasn't returned.

Maybe the store in town didn't have his cleaner, and he had to drive somewhere farther away. Perhaps his truck broke down or he ran out of gas. Or maybe he got into a car accident and died.

Each option is equally as frustrating given the context of our situation.

Maybe he's gone to the police station to turn me in. But no, he wouldn't do that. He can't. Not when he's committed more crimes than I have. Not when I can spin my involvement as coercion of a minor. He can't do *anything* without incriminating himself. I'd kill him if he tried. And I would make him suffer more than all those girls combined.

I stare at the old grandfather clock, again, and see that only a minute has passed.

It's going to be a long day.

\*\*\*

He's finally back.

I get up off the couch and greet him at the door. His hands are full of the various items he purchased, most of which look like useless junk. I take the jug of cleaning solution from him and examine it. Before I get a chance to look, though, he yanks it from my hands.

"Hey!"

He scowls at me in response and marches

into the kitchen. I follow behind him, hearing a *thud* when he drops the jug and other items onto the kitchenette table.

"What's wrong with you?" I ask, jokingly.

"Stop talking."

He doesn't yell it, but there's an authority in his tone that makes me oblige.

I didn't think he'd be this mad about Sylvia. I had hoped that he'd never find out about her in the first place, but still. This seems like an overreaction.

"Here's what's going to happen. You're going to ride your bike home. And I'm going to stay here and clean up your mess."

"What? It's like, a two-hour drive to get there. Do you know how long it'll take on a bike?"

"Stop talking," he repeats. "It's still light outside. Stay on the side of the road and ride your bike until you're home. Take a bath or a shower and change out of those dirty clothes."

I look down and realize that I'm still wearing my clothes from last night.

"Throw the clothes in the garbage, but not our garbage. Find a dumpster behind a store nearby and throw them in there. Those clothes, and what's on them, are incriminating pieces of evidence. Get. Rid. Of. Them."

He looks as if he's harbouring an ungodly amount of rage and, for a moment, I wonder if he'll try to kill me. These instructions could just be a part of some elaborate plan to get me in a vulnerable position. To eliminate me from the equation.

There's only been one other time when I genuinely thought that he might kill me, and that was when I first caught him in the act. I saw that look in his eyes, the gaze of him contemplating his options. That's when I told him to let me help. I didn't barter with him to save my life, but the deal we struck very well could have spared me.

"Go. Now."

He speaks in staccato.

"When will you be home?"

I get no response and decide to leave. He goes into the storage shed to get out my old bicycle, and I take the opportunity to seize one of the kitchen knives to take with me. Just in case.

When he returns, he tells me that the bike is out front, waiting for me. Then he disappears into the basement with the cleaning supplies.

As promised, my bicycle is out front, flopped onto the grass. I contemplate bringing the kitchen knife with me for the ride but decide against it. I have no pockets, no backpack to put it in. And I certainly can't ride around with a knife in my hand.

I toss the knife on the lawn and head down the dirt road.

I don't look back.

# NOW

May 12th, 1970
3:17 pm.

It was past three o'clock when the nurses finally let me go.

"You're one lucky lady for getting out of there when you did," one nurse had told me.

"Victor Cobb is about as dangerous as they come," the other agreed.

I leave the prison with a bandage on my face and a lollipop for good measure. It's pouring rain and the sky is a dark gray, despite it being the afternoon. I half-run through the parking lot to my car, unsuccessfully avoiding puddles along the way. By the time I unlock the door, my feet are soaked – but not even soggy loafers can wipe the smile off of my face.

I've waited years to meet with him, face to face, and I finally did it. More importantly, I got more than enough information for this to be the headlining interview for my book. I stick the key in the ignition and drive away, not bothering to look back at the building I'm leaving behind. Good riddance.

Somehow, the sky gets darker. My wipers struggle to repel the raindrops bombarding my windshield, so I drive faster. I'll be home quicker this way. God, I cannot wait to get out of this rain and these wet clothes so that I can start writing his segment. I have so much information to choose from, I don't know how I'll ever fit it all into one book. Part of me wishes that I hadn't already interviewed Walter Gordon and Kassem Zhao and the Black Widow, and even little Lee Jenkins, just so I could have a whole text dedicated to Victor Cobb.

Thunder strikes one, two, three times, the pavement shaking beneath my car. Only it's not thunder; it's the sound of my car veering off the road and crashing into the guard rail.

Everything goes black, as black as the sky.

# NOW

May 17th, 1970
*Morning*

The worst migraine I've ever had wakes me from the best sleep I've ever had.

Harsh fluorescent lights meet my gaze when I open my eyes, making my headache worse. I try to turn onto my side, away from the lights, but can't. I'm hooked up to a bunch of shit and can't move. I wriggle around in the bed, wanting to free myself.

I have an overwhelming need to get fresh air.

Loud noises begin to sound around me, and amid my

thrashing, I see that they're coming from machinery. Hospital machines. I'm in a hospital.

A nurse comes barreling into my room with a few others trailing close behind her.

"Air," I gasp, "I need air."

"Sorry, Hunny. There ain't no windows in this room. You're gonna have to wait a bit."

Another nurse playfully punches the one who spoke.

"Hush now," she says.

I repeat myself. "I need fresh air."

My words come out raspier than the first time, and I can hardly make sense of them. Nobody pays me any attention, though. They're all too concerned with the beeping machines to worry about their patient struggling to breathe. So, I scream. I've been doing a lot of screaming lately.

I thrash wildly and scream louder than I ever have, rotating my head in every direction to make sure everyone gets their fair share of my screeching.

"Good Lord, she is wailing like a banshee," a nurse says, to no one in particular.

I'm not exactly sure when I started to cry, but I'm crying. I haven't cried real tears in years.

I stop screaming but I don't know why. I want to keep screaming but my throat feels constricted, and my mind feels sleepy. I look down just in time to see a sedative being put in my IV.

# NOW

May 19th, 1970
*8:12 pm.*

When I wake up this time around, I don't scream. I don't do anything; I just lay in the hospital bed and think.

I keep coming back to one thought, and that's Sylvia. The real one. I don't know what made her so special in comparison to all of his other victims, but I had an attachment to her. She was kind and beautiful and sarcastic, despite the circumstances. I wish I could have saved her.

But I couldn't have saved her because I'm the one who killed her. And she wasn't his victim; she was mine. All mine.

I haven't allowed that thought to pass through the stone barriers of my mind. It wasn't true because I didn't acknowledge it. If her body wasn't ever found, and no one was ever convicted, then did Sylvia really die?

For years, I convinced myself that the answer is no. But I see things clearly now, and the real answer is yes. Sylvia died and I was the one with my hands around her throat; the one with a rock in my hand smashing her skull to smithereens.

I think I'm finally ready to accept that.

# NOW

May 21st, 1970
9:02 am.

"My name is Sylvia St. James," I tell the doctor, upon waking up from my sedation.

I also killed Sylvia St. James, but I keep that bit to myself.

To test the potential impact the crash had on my memory, Dr. Palmer quizzes me on various facts about myself, which really aren't facts about me at all.

"When is your date of birth, Miss St. James?"

"November 13th, 1947." But it's actually March 23rd.

"What year is it?"

"It's 1970."

"Good, good."

Palmer writes some notes on his clipboard and deems me stable enough to be discharged.

It's been over a week since the accident, and I've been itching to get home ever since. After my initial meltdown, I had some time to reflect on myself as Sylvia St. James. I also thought about what life would be like if I were Evie Cobb again.

Seven years ago, after Sylvia was dead, my father had taken out Sylvia's identification cards from her cheap purse. That way, it would be more difficult to identify Sylvia if her remains were ever found. They weren't. Sylvia's abduction and murder were the only crimes my father was never charged with, probably because her body was never found. That, and the fact that he was only an accessory to murder in that case.

To this day, I still don't know where he buried Sylvia, or if he did even bury her. And as far as the law is concerned, Sylvia St. James is a runaway teen who never came home.

After that was all taken care of, my father confessed to the murder of six girls, and the police arrested him. My mother was heartbroken when she heard the news, and felt awful for me because I lost my father. "It could have been you," she kept saying. She never found out the truth about my involvement and she never will.

A few years after my father was put away, I figured I

was in the clear. I took the driver's license and birth certificate, and I became Sylvia. Seriously, who the hell carries their birth certificate on them, anyway? Serves her right.

When I turned eighteen and moved out, I travelled to Toronto and formally assumed her identity. I don't know why. I don't feel pity for her or regret for what I've done, and I'm not trying to carry on her legacy.

After hours and hours of thought, I determined that it might be because I was ashamed.

Ashamed of my true nature, of who I am. But I realize now that I have no reason to be ashamed.

And I know exactly what I need to do.

# NOW

May 21st, 1970
12:25 pm.

I'm finally home after my stint in the hospital, and I can't wait to carry out my plans.

I set down my purse and unlock the door. When I step into my apartment, I smell something putrid, which causes me to take a few steps back. After a moment, I enter hesitantly, plugging my nose, and turn on the lights. The first thing I see is Candy lying on the floor near his food and water dish, both of which are empty. I think he's dead. It definitely smells like he's dead.

The scent of his decaying corpse is spoiling my return home, so I grab a garbage bag from underneath the sink and toss Candy inside.

Now *that's* some sour candy.

The living room still smells over an hour later, despite the source having been disposed of.

I was going to do some brainstorming for the finalization of my book but decided to pack my bags instead. I close the door after entering my bedroom to keep out the smell, not that that makes any difference at this point. I toss the luggage I brought out from the closet onto my bed and get to work.

I bring out all of my favourite clothes and shoes and shove as many of them as I can fit into the suitcase. I also pack some books that I like, such as *Lolita* and *Crime and Punishment*. I bring the secret leather journal I took from my old bedroom and put it in with my books, too. I think it might come in handy.

I move the packing party into the washroom, where I gather all of my makeup and toiletries. Most importantly, I lift a loose floor tile and retrieve my passport, birth certificate, beginner's license, health card, and social security number. My real ones, with my real name. I toss them into my purse and return to the living room to finish packing.

The smell takes me back once more, but I've accepted the stench. It won't be much longer now, anyways.

I round up the belongings at my desk, which largely

consist of notes and inmate & case files for my book. After carefully laying them flat in a special compartment in my luggage, I close the case to my portable typewriter and bring that with me, too.

This is it.

I feel like I'm forgetting something, but maybe that's because I'm only now realizing how few belongings I have. I don't have any pictures on my walls or photo albums on the shelves, and there aren't any knick-knacks or sentimental decor. No gifts, either. There were those flowers that Damian gave me that are still on the floor, but they're wilted and dead like Candy now.

I leave my apartment and don't look back. I think about saying goodbye to Damian, but then he would expect an apology for recording the meeting with his cousin, Lee. I'm not sorry, though, and I don't particularly have the energy to falsify an apology, so I won't. I say a silent goodbye to him in my head.

As I walk down the many flights of stairs, dragging my suitcase behind me, I also think about seeing my mother before I go. But would she even care? I don't care, and she probably won't, so it's a no-go for my mother, too. I'm especially pissed at her, so I give her a large mental "fuck you".

I reach the main floor and exit the building for what's likely the last time. I put my luggage and typewriter into the trunk of my rental car and find myself smiling as I do so. I feel like I'm free from the chains of Sylvia, and there's only one person I want to see before I go.

\*\*\*

When I get to the prison, I sign my name on the visitor's list:

**NAME:** Evie Cobb
**RELATIONSHIP TO INMATE:** Daughter

# NOW

May 21st, 1970
1:12 pm.

"You're back," my father says.
"Evidently."
"Have you come to apologize?"
My eye roll and scowl speak for me.
"Alright, then," he continues. "What do you want, *Sylvia*?"
"Call me Evie."
"What?"
"You heard me the first time. I'm not repeating it."

"But, why? What changed?"

"I decided I didn't want to live in her shadow anymore. I don't want to hide myself from the world – my true self. Because the truth is that I don't have personal relationships and I don't want any. And if a child falls and hurts themselves, I laugh. I'm tired of pretending that things like that aren't funny when they are. It's fucking hilarious watching little Billy ball his eyes out, crying for his mommy, pounding his fists on the ground when he spills his ice cream cone or trips and scrapes his knee."

"You're twisted, Evie. You're sick."

"That's rich, coming from the man who murdered six teenage girls."

"I'm not innocent, I know that. But I didn't take pleasure in killing them. It was the lesser of two evils. If it wasn't them, it would have been you. I loved you and didn't want to see you hurt, no matter how angry you made me. I knew, deep down, that it wasn't your fault."

"That's bullshit and you know it," I spit.

"Perhaps. Believe me or don't, it's not my problem anymore. Really, though. Why did you come here? Are you going to throw another conniption fit and get me sent to solitary for a day?"

"No. I'm skipping town, probably for good. You could say that I've had an epiphany. I don't want the anonymity of the city anymore. I've freed myself from the confinement of Sylvia's identity and now I want to explore myself as Evie. I suppose I just wanted to tell you before I left."

"So, you wanted to say goodbye?"

"I just wanted to let you know that I'm leaving."

"Well, you've let me know," he sighs.

I stand up and smooth my plaid skirt a few times before making my departure. At the last second, though, I turn around and look my father in the eye.

"Goodbye, dad."

**TWO YEARS LATER**

# NOW

October 12th, 1972
8:34 pm.

I finish raking the leaves into a gargantuan pile and shove my bare hands into the sleeves of my coat. It's really damn cold.

The upkeep and renovation have been overwhelming since moving into the old farmhouse, but it's kept me busy. I didn't have electricity for the first few months, but after I got the advance for publishing my book, I made enough money to keep the lights on, and then some.

*Monsters Are Human, Too* made its publication debut

in June of last year, and it topped the charts in the non-fiction category for the entire summer. It's still doing pretty well, but I think my current project is going to be even better. I'm working with the same publishing house in Toronto to publish another book, but this time, it's fiction.

My book follows a young girl, Kate, and her father, Jeb, who happens to be a murderer. Jeb kills teenage girls in his spare time and has been getting away with it for years; that is until Kate walks in on him. Jeb is about to kill his daughter when he decides to use her as his lackey instead. Kate is forced to assist her father in killing these girls, but eventually, she learns to love the art of murder.

Completely fictive, of course.

My publisher loved the initial pitch and thought it would be a great segue into the world of fiction. I've been working on the manuscript for a few months now, and the farmhouse serves as the perfect writing location. It's secluded, remote, and bears a strong resemblance to the setting of my novel, that's most definitely a made-up story.

I toss the rake onto the browning grass and walk around to the rear of the property. The pond looks desolate, and all the plants are dead. I think I like the farmhouse better in the autumn when it's dreary, but the ground is still visible. Winters are a different story; the snow is awful here.

The chill air nips at my exposed skin and I head inside to make a steaming pot of coffee.

I've had all the hardwood floors restored, at least on the main floor. I repainted the living room and tore down the fruit & vegetable wallpaper in the kitchen, replacing it with a cream coat of paint. Most of the original furniture is still here, but I got an all-new set for my bedroom once I had the money. A canopy bed and matching oak dresser, a moss-green bedspread and a dark armchair. I even got a small writing desk to put in the corner, just in case inspiration hits in the middle of the night, as it so often does.

My main office is in the room next-door, though. I recently installed floor-to-ceiling bookshelves lining one full wall, with my desk facing away from the window at the back of the room. I moved my mother's stained-glass lamp from downstairs up onto my desk, and I took the dining room's area rug, too.

There are still things that need to be done, like repaving the outdoor walkway or re-shingling the roof or finishing the backyard expansion into the surrounding brush, but the house is really coming together.

I like to think that I've changed for the better since I ditched the Sylvia alias and accepted myself for who I am, and what I've done. Moving into the farmhouse full-time has allowed me the luxury of isolation, something that Toronto didn't give me. I did a lot of self-reflection and truly came to terms with who I am, and what I want to do with my life.

As of now, I never plan on leaving this farmhouse.

I stir my coffee and swirl it around in my mug when I hear a suspicious noise. The pitter-patter almost sounds like footsteps, but that can't be true. I grab a butcher's knife from the kitchen drawer and set my coffee on the table. The noise happens again, but this time, it sounds as if it were coming from above me. I creep up the stairs and trail the noise until I'm outside one of the bedrooms, the door closed tight. Without hesitation, I burst through the door and scare the poor thing. The cat hisses and scurries out of the room between my legs, and then down the stairs. It was only Candy II.

Funny enough, about a month or so after moving into the farmhouse, I saw a cat hanging out on the porch. He wasn't on his deathbed like Candy was when I found him outside my apartment years ago, but he certainly wasn't in great health, either. I slapped a collar on him and dubbed him Candy II. He's a gray mancoon cat with no physical resemblance to the first Candy, but the name just seemed fitting.

I follow Candy II down the stairs and resume my cup of coffee until I hear another sound. This time, I know undoubtedly what it is. I leave my coffee once again and head into the basement, which I haven't touched during my two years of renovations.

When I reach the bottom of the stairs, I pull the light-bulb string, illuminating the room with a dull glow.

She stops clinking her chains when she sees me and crawls into the corner instead.

"What, are you scared?" I mock. The girl nods her head fervently, eyes wild with adrenaline. "I don't care how damned scared you are. Shut up and stop that nonsense with your chains. It's pointless."

I give the girl a curt nod and go back upstairs.

I don't know who the girl is, and I don't care. Many have worn those chains before her, and many more will bear them after she's dead. I've kept her alive longer than the others, but not because I want to. I need to finish up the yard expansion so that I have more square footage for my gardens, and for what I bury beneath them.

She'll be dead within a week, nonetheless.

This is me, Evie Cobb. Daughter and accomplice of the murderer Victor Cobb. Solo murderer of eight girls and counting. My father may claim to have killed for my sake, my safety. Maybe he did, maybe he didn't. He says he killed for me, but I'll never know for sure. What I do know is that my murders aren't for him, or anybody else. The first kill that I assisted my father with was scary and thrilling and not entirely of my own volition. I proposed our deal but didn't truly understand what it meant until we were finished.

That first kill was for him. Every one after that?

I did it for me.

I *do* it for me.

# ACKNOWLEDGMENTS

I'm overjoyed to be writing the acknowledgments section of my debut novel, *I Did It For You.*

First, I'd like to thank every member of my immediate and extended family who has supported me and this book, as well as the short story collection that came before it. The success of *Bird Boy: and Other Short Stories* and the support I received from my family were critical to my growth as a writer. Most significantly, your love and support helped me to build my confidence. I published *Bird Boy* with the intent of just having a piece of my writing out there. I didn't expect to sell more than five copies (seriously; my goal was five copies). I thought that those five sales, if I got them, would be from pity or obligation. This time around, I published *I Did It For You* with confidence, pride, and the knowledge that I am loved and supported on my journey as a writer. For every grandparent, aunt, uncle, cousin, second cousin, family friend, and anyone with even a remote familial relation to me, thank you. Your support is what made this book possible.

That includes my parents, to who I also want to give a thank-you. You raised a child who loved to read and helped foster that love into a passion for literature. Growing up, you always asserted that I could do anything that I want to; be anything that I want to. When I was ten years old, I wanted to be an author, and today, I am an author. Special shout-out to my Dadager (dad-manager, duh). Thank you.

My coworkers and management team at the bookstore in which I work at have been incredibly supportive of my writing endeavors. Thank you to each and every one of you who has bought or read one of my books, recommended it to a customer, or who has simply given me words of encouragement. It means the world! A special thank you to my coworker, Ally, my unofficial agent, fangirl, and friend.

This thank-you goes to you, the reader. Whether I know you personally or not, thank you. Whether you're family or a stranger, an old friend or a friend-of-a-friend, thank you, thank you, thank you. It's always scary releasing my work into the world for anyone to read, but I have received tremendous support on my social media channels from readers of *Bird Boy*. I hope that you enjoyed *I Did It For You*, as well, and I'd love to hear your thoughts. Thank you for supporting me and my book. I appreciate it beyond words.

I'd also like to shout out the array of documentaries and television shows that first inspired my interest in true crime and criminal psychology. *Criminal Minds, Hannibal, Prodigal Son, Night Stalker: The Hunt For a Serial Killer*, just to name a few.

My cliche "and last but not least" thanks goes to my

partner, Ethan. You supported me through the worst times of my life and celebrated alongside me during the highest times. You also act as the best proofreader, beta-reader, and listener there is. The best part is that I don't even have to pay! In all seriousness, though, you've been with me every step of the way in my writing career, and the creation of *I Did It For You* is no exception. For a whole year, I didn't stop talking about it. No, really; it would probably be annoying to just about anyone else, but not you. I excessively talked about this book during every stage of the process because I was so excited, and you supported me with it and matched my enthusiasm. To my very first reader, my best friend, and the person that I love, thank you so much.

That's it! Hopefully, I didn't forget to thank anyone. Once more, I give my utmost thanks, gratitude, and love to everyone who supports me and my books. I'll see you for my next release!

# ABOUT THE AUTHOR

**JORDAN MURRAY** is a writer from Toronto, Canada. At just 19 years old, she published a collection of short fiction titled, *Bird Boy: and Other Short Stories,* which went on to top an Amazon Bestseller's list. At 21 years old, she published her debut novel, *I Did It For You*, which she wrote when she was 20 years old. Jordan always has ideas and projects in the works and is no doubt already working on the next novel. And the one after that. And maybe a side project or two in between.

**JORDAN** is an avid reader. She loves reading suspense thrillers, horror, romance, fantasy, young adult, manga … you get the gist. Being an English major also means that she is quite familiarized with the likes of classic literature. Jordan has been playing the piano since she was twelve years old, and has also dabbled in vocals, violin, and guitar. Her love of music partially inspired the short story "Ostinato" in her first collection of short fiction, *Bird Boy.*

Manufactured by Amazon.ca
Bolton, ON